Philip K. Dick was born in Chicago in 1928 and lived most of his life in California. He attended college for a year at Berkeley. Apart from writing, his main interest was music: at one time he ran a record shop and also a classical music programme for a local radio station. He won the Hugo Award for his classic novel of alternative history, *The Man in the High Castle* (1962). He was married five times and had three children. He died in March 1982.

'Dick quietly produced serious fiction in a popular form and there can be no greater praise'
Michael Moorcock

'One of the most original practitioners writing any kind of fiction, Philip K. Dick made most of the European avant-garde seem navel-gazers in a cul-de-sac'
Sunday Times

'No other writer of his generation had such a powerful intellectual presence. He has stamped himself not only on our memories but in our imagination'
Brian Aldiss

'The most consistently brilliant SF writer in the world'
John Brunner

By the same author

Novels

Solar Lottery
Eye in the Sky
Vulcan's Hammer
The Man who Japed
The Cosmic Puppets
The World Jones Made
Time Out of Joint
Dr Futurity
*The Man in the High
    Castle*
The Game Players of Titan
Clans of the Alphane Moon
*Flow My Tears, the
    Policeman Said*
The Penultimate Truth
The Simulacra
Martian Time-Slip
*Dr Bloodmoney or How
    We Got Along After the
    Bomb*
The Unteleported Man
Now Wait for Last Year
Counter-Clock World
Blade Runner (also
    published as *Do
    Androids Dream of
    Electric Sheep?*)
Ubik
Our Friends from Frolix 8

Galactic Pot-Healer
*The Three Stigmata of
    Palmer Eldritch*
A Scanner Darkly
Valis
The Divine Invasion
*The Transmigration of
    Timothy Archer*
*Confessions of a Crap
    Artist*
The Ganymede Takeover
    (with Ray Nelson)
Deus Irae (with Roger
    Zelazny)
A Maze of Death
Lies, Inc.
*The Man Whose Teeth
    Were All Exactly Alike*
In Milton Lumky Territory
*Puttering About in a
    Small Land*
Radio Free Albemuth

Short Stories

A Handful of Darkness
The Variable Man
The Preserving Machine
The Book of Philip K. Dick
The Golden Man

PHILIP K. DICK

The Zap Gun

*Being that Most Excellent Account of Travails
and Contayning Many Pretie Hystories By Him
Set Foorth in Comely Colours and Most Delight-
fully Discoursed Upon As Beautified and Well
Furnished Divers Good and Commendable in the
Gesiht of Men of That Most Lamentable Wepens
Fasoun Designer Lars Powderdry and What Nearly
Became of Him Due to Certain Most Dreadful
Forces*

GRAFTON BOOKS

A Division of the Collins Publishing Group

LONDON GLASGOW
TORONTO SYDNEY AUCKLAND

Grafton Books
A Division of the Collins Publishing Group
8 Grafton Street, London W1X 3LA

First published in Great Britain by
Grafton Books 1975
Reprinted 1978, 1984, 1986

ISBN 0-586-04112-5

Printed and bound in Great Britain by
Collins, Glasgow

Set in Linotype Plantin

The guidance-system of weapons-item 207, which consists of six hundred miniaturized electronic components, can best be plow-shared as a lacquered ceramic owl which appears to the unenlightened only as an ornament; the informed knowing, however, that the owl's head, when removed, reveals a hollow body in which cigars or pencils can be stored.

Official report of the UN-W Natsec Board of
Wesbloc, October 5, 2003, by Concomody A
(true identity for security reasons not to be given
out; vide Board rulings XV 4–5–6–7–8).

ONE

'Mr. Lars, sir.'

'I'm afraid I only have a moment to talk to your viewers. Sorry.' He started on, but the autonomic TV interviewer, camera in its hand, blocked his path. The metal smile of the creature glittered confidently.

'You feel a trance coming on, sir?' the autonomic interviewer inquired hopefully, as if perhaps such could take place before one of the multifax alternate lens-systems of its portable camera.

Lars Powderdry sighed. From where he stood on the footers' runnel he could see his New York office. See, but not reach it. Too many people – the pursaps! – were interested in *him*, not his work And the work of course was all that mattered.

He said wearily, 'The time factor. Don't you understand? In the world of weapons fashions —'

'Yes, we hear you're receiving something really spectacular,' the autonomic interviewer gushed, picking up the thread of discourse without even salutationary attention to Lars' own meaning. 'Four trances in *one* week. And it's almost come all the way through! Correct, Mr. Lars, sir?'

The autonomic construct was an idiot. Patiently he tried to make it understand. He did not bother to address himself to the legion of pursaps, mostly ladies, who viewed this early-morning show – *Lucky Bagman Greets You*, or whatever it was called. Lord knew *he* didn't know. He had no time in his workday for such witless diversions as this. 'Look,' he said, this time gently, as if the autonomic interviewer were really

7

alive and not merely an arbitrarily endowed sentient concoction of the ingenuity of Wes-block technology of A.D. 2004. Ingenuity, he reflected, wasted in this direction ... although, on a closer thought, was this so much more an abomination than his own field? A reflection unpleasant to consider.

He repressed it from his mind and said, 'In weapons fashions an item must arise at a certain time. Tomorrow, next week or next month is too late.'

'Tell us what it is,' the interviewer said, and hung with bated avidity on the anticipated answer. How could anyone, even Mr. Lars of New York and Paris, disappoint all the millions of viewers throughout Wes-bloc, in a dozen countries? To let them down would be to serve the interests of Peep-East, or so the autonomic interviewer wished to convey. But it was failing.

Lars said, 'It's frankly none of your business.' And stalked past the small bunch of footers who had assembled to gawk, stalked away from the warm glow of instant-exposure before public observation and to the up-track of Mr. Lars, Incorporated, the single-story structure arranged as if by intention among high-rise offices whose size alone announced the essential nature of their function.

Physical size, Lars reflected as he reached the outer, public lobby of Mr. Lars, Incorporated, was a false criterion. Even the autonomic interviewer wasn't fooled; it was Lars Powderdry that it wished to expose to its audience, not the industrial entities within easy reach. However much the entities would have delighted in seeing their ak-prop – acquisition-propaganda – experts thundering into the attentive ears of its audience.

The doors of Mr. Lars, Incorporated, shut, tuned as they were to his own cephalic pattern. He sealed off, safe from the gaping multitude whose attention had been jazzed up by professionals. On their own the pursaps whould have been reasonable about it; that is, they would be apathetic.

'Mr. Lars.'

'Yes, Miss Bedouin.' He halted. 'I know. The drafting department can't make head or tail of sketch 285.' To that he

8

was resigned. Having seen it himself, after Friday's trance, he knew how muddied it was.

'Well, they said —' She hesitated, young and small, ill-equipped temperamentally to carry the grievances of others around in her possession as their spokesman.

'I'll talk to them direct,' he said to her humanely. 'Frankly, to me it looked like a self-programming eggbeater mounted on triangular wheels.' And what can you destroy, he reflected, with that?

'Oh, they seem to feel it's a fine weapon,' Miss Bedouin said, her natural, hormone-enriched breasts moving in synchronicity with his notice of them. 'I believe they just can't make out the power source. You know, the erg structure. Before you go to 286 —'

'They want me,' he said, 'to take a better look at 285. Okay.' It did not bother him. He felt amiably inclined, because this was a pleasant April day and Miss Bedouin (or, if you liked to think about it that way, Miss Bed) was pretty enough to restore any man's sanguineness. Even a fashion designer – a weapons fashion designer.

Even, he thought, the best and only weapons fashion designer in all Wes-bloc.

To turn up his equal – and even this was in doubt, as far as he was concerned – one would have to approach that other hemisphere, Peep-East. The Sino-Soviet bloc owned or employed or however they handled it – in any case had available to them – services of a medium like himself.

He had often wondered about her. Her name was Miss Topchev, the planet-wide private police agency KACH had informed him. Lilo Topchev. With only one office, and that at Bulganingrad rather than New Moscow.

She sounded reclusive to him, but KACH did not orate on subjective aspects of its scrutiny-targets. Perhaps, he thought, Miss Topchev knitted her weapons sketches ... or made them up, while still in the trance-state, in the form of gaily colored ceramic tile. Anyhow, something artistic. Whether her client – or more accurately employer – the Peep-East governing body SeRKeb, that grim, uncolored and unadorned holistic academy of cogs, against which his own hemisphere had for so many decades now pitted every resource within itself, liked it or not.

Because of course a weapons fashion designer had to be catered to. In his own career he had managed to establish that.

After all, he could not be compelled to enter his five-days-a-week trance. And probably neither could Lilo Topchev.

Leaving Miss Bedouin, he entered his own office, removing his outer cape, cap and slippers, and extended these discarded items of street-wear to the handicloset.

Already his medical team, Dr. Todt and nurse Elvira Funt, had sighted him. They rose and approached respectfully, and with them his near-psionically gifted quasi-subordinate, Henry Morris. One never knew – he thought, constructing their reasoning on the basis of their alert, alarmed manner – when a trance might come on. Nurse Funt had her intravenous machinery tagging hummingly behind her and Dr. Todt, a first-class product of the superior West German medical world, stood ready to whip out delicate devices for two distinct purposes: first, that no cardiac arrest during the trance-state occur, no infarcts to the lungs or excessive suppression of the vagus nerve, causing cessation of breathing and hence suffocation, and second – and without this there was no point to it all – that mentation during the trance-state be established in a permanent record, obtainable after the state had ended.

Dr. Todt was, therefore, essential in the business at Mr. Lars, Incorporated. At the Paris office a similar, equally skilled crew awaited on stand-by. Because it often happened that Lars Powderdry got a more powerful emanation at that locus than he did in hectic New York.

And in addition his mistress Maren Faine lived and worked there.

It was a weakness – or, as he preferred supposing, a strength of weapons fashion designers, in contrast to their miserable counterparts in the world of clothing – that they liked women. His predecessor, Wade, had been heterosexual, too – had in fact killed himself over a little coloratura of the Dresden

10

Festival ensemble. Mr. Wade had suffered auricular fibrillation at an ignoble time: while in bed at the girl's Vienna condominium apartment at two in the morning, long after *The Marriage of Figaro* had dropped curtain, and Rita Grandi had discarded the silk hose, blouse, etc., for – as the alert homeopape pics had disclosed – nothing.

So, at forty-three years of age, Mr Wade, the previous weapons fashion designer for Wes-bloc, had left the scene – and left vacant his essential post. But there were others ready to emerge and replace him.

Perhaps that had hurried Mr. Wade. The job itself was taxing – medical science did not precisely know to what degree or how. And there was, Lars Powderdry reflected, nothing quite so disorienting as knowing that not only are you indispensable but that simultaneously you can be replaced. It was the sort of paradox that no one enjoyed, except of course UN-W Natsec, the governing Board of Wes-bloc, who had contrived to keep a replacement always visible in the wings.

He thought, And they've probably got another one waiting right now.

They *like* me, he thought. They've been good to me and I to them; the system functions.

But ultimate authorities, in charge of the lives of billions of pursaps, don't take risks. They do not cross against the DON'T WALK signs of cog life.

Not that the pursaps would relieve them of their posts ... hardly. Removal would *descend*, from General George McFarlane Nitz, the C. in C. on Natsec's Board. Nitz could remove anyone. In fact if the necessity (or perhaps merely the opportunity) arose to remove himself – imagine the satisfaction of disarming his own person, stripping himself of the brain-pan i.d. unit that caused him to smell right to the autonomic sentries which guarded Festung Washington!

And frankly, considering the cop-like aura of General Nitz, the Supreme Hatchet-man implications of his —

'Your blood-pressure, Mr. Lars.' Narrow, priest-like, somber Dr. Todt advanced, machinery in tow. 'Please, Lars.'

Beyond Dr. Todt and nurse Elvira Funt a slim, bald, pale-as-straw but highly professional-looking young man in peasoup green rose, a folio under his arm. Lars Powderdry at once beckoned to him. Blood-pressure readings could wait. This was the fella from KACH, and he had something with him.

'May we go into your private office, Mr. Lars?' the KACH-man asked.

Leading the way Lars said, 'Photos.'

'Yes, sir.' The KACH-man shut the office door carefully after them. 'Of her sketches of —' he opened the folio, examined a Xeroxed document – 'last Wednesday. Their codex AA-335.' Finding a vacant spot on Lars' desk he began spreading out the stereo pics. 'Plus one blurred shot of a mockup at the Rostok Academy assembly-lab ... of —' Again he consulted his poop sheet – 'SeRKeb codex AA-330.' He stood aside so that Lars could inspect.

Seating himself Lars lit a Cuesta Rey astoria and did not inspect. He felt his wits become turgid, and the cigar did not help. He did not enjoy snooping dog-like over spy-obtained pics of the output of his Peep-East equivalent, Miss Topchev. Let UN-W Natsec do the analysis! He had so much as said this to General Nitz on several occasions, once at a meeting of the total Board, with everyone present sunk within his most dignified and stately presgarms – his prestige capes, miter, boots, gloves ... probably spider-silk underwear with ominous slogans and ukases, stitched in multicolored thread.

There, in that solemn environment, with the burden of Atlas on the backs of even the concomodies – those six drafted, involuntary fools – in formal session, Lars had mildly asked that for Chrissakes couldn't they do the analysis of the enemy's weapons?

No. And without debate. Because (listen closely, Mr. Lars) these are not Peep-East's weapons. These are his *plans* for weapons. We will evaluate them when they've passed from prototype to autofac production, General Nitz had intoned. But as regards this initial stage ... he had eyed Lars meaningfully.

Lighting an old fashioned – and illegal – cigarette, the pale, bald young KACH-man murmured, 'Mr. Lars, we have something more. It may not interest you, but since you seem to be waiting anyhow ...'

He dipped deep into the folio.

Lars said, 'I'm waiting because I hate this. Not because I want to see any more. God forbid.'

'Umm.' The KACH-man brought forth an additional eight-by-ten glossy and leaned back.

It was a non-stereo pic – taken from a great distance, possibly even from an eye-spy, satellite, then severely processed – of Lilo Topchev.

TWO

'Oh, yes,' Lars said with vast caution. 'I asked for that, didn't I?' Unofficially, of course. As a favor by KACH to him personally, with absolutely nothing in writing – with what the old-timers called 'a calculated risk.' 'You can't tell too much from this,' the KACH-man admitted.

'I can't tell anything.' Lars glared, baffled.

The KACH-man shrugged with professional nonchalance, and said, 'We'll try again. You see, she never goes anywhere or does anything. They don't let her. It may be just a cover-story, but they say her trance-states tend to come on involuntarily, in a pseudo-epileptoid pattern. Possibly drug-induced, is our guess off the record, of course. They don't want her to fall down in the middle of the public runnels and be flattened by one of their old surface vehicles.'

'You mean they don't want her to bolt to Wes-bloc.'

The KACH-man gestured philosophically.

'Am I right?' Lars asked.

'Afraid not. Miss Topchev is paid a salary equal to that of

13

the prime mover of SeRKeb, Marshal Paponovich. She has a top-floor, high-rise view conapt, a maid, butler, Mercedes-Benz hovercar. As long as she cooperates —'

'From this pic,' Lars said, 'I can't even tell how old she is. Let alone what she looked like.'

'Lilo Topchev is twenty-three.'

The office door opened and short, sloppy, unpunctual, on-the-brink-of-being-relieved-of-his-position but essential Henry Morris conjured himself into their frame of reference. 'Anything for me?'

Lars said, 'Come here.' He indicated the pic of Lilo Topchev.

Swiftly the KACH-man restored the pic to its folio. 'Classified, Mr. Lars! 20-20. You know; for your eyes alone.'

Lars said, 'Mr. Morris is my eyes.' This was, evidently, one of KACH's more difficult functionaries. 'What is your name?' Lars asked him, and held his pen ready at a notepad.

After a pause the KACH-man relaxed. 'An ipse dixit, but — do whatever you wish with the pic, Mr. Lars.' He returned it to the desk, no expression on his sunless, expert face. Henry Morris came around to bend over it, squinting and scowling, his fleshy jowls wobbling as he visibly masticated, as if trying to ingest something of substance from the blurred pic.

The vidcom on Lars' desk pinged and his secretary Miss Grabhorn said, 'Call from the Paris office. Miss Faine herself, I believe.' The most minuscule trace of disapproval in her voice, a tiny coldness.

'Excuse me,' Lars said to the KACH-man. But then, still holding his pen poised, he said, 'Let's have your name anyhow. Just for the record. In the rare case I might want to get in touch with you again.'

The KACH-man, as if revealing something foul, said reluctantly, 'I'm Don Packard, Mr. Lars.' He fussed with his hands. The question made him oddly ill-at-ease.

After writing this down, Lars fingered the vidcom to *on* and the face of his mistress lit, illuminated from within like some fair, dark-haired jack-o-lantern. 'Lars!'

'Maren!' His tone was of fondness, not cruelty. Maren

Faine always aroused his protective instincts. And yet she annoyed him in the fashion that a loved child might. Maren never knew when to stop.

'Busy?'

'Yeah.'

'Are you flying to Paris this afternoon? We can have dinner together and then, oh my God, there's this *gleckik* blue jazz combo —'

'Jazz isn't blue,' Lars said. 'It's pale green.' He glanced at Henry Morris. 'Isn't jazz a very pale green?' Henry nodded.

Angrily, Maren Faine said. 'You make me wish —'

'I'll call you back.' Lars said to her. 'Dear.' He shut down the vidcom. 'I'll look at the weapons sketches now,' he said to the KACH-man. Meanwhile, narrow Dr. Todt and nurse Elvira Funt had entered his office unannounced; reflexively he extended his arm for the first blood-pressure reading of the day, as Don Packard rearranged the sketches and began to point out details which seemed meaningful to the police agency's own very second-rate privately maintained weapons analysts.

Work, at Mr. Lars, Incorporated, had on this day, in this manner, begun. It was, somehow, Lars thought, not encouraging. He was disappointed at the useless pic of Miss Topchev; perhaps that had summoned his mood of pessimism. Or was there more to come?

He had, at ten a.m. New York time, an appointment with General Nitz' rep, a colonel named – God, what *was* his name? Anyhow, at that time Lars would receive the Board's reaction to the last batch of mockups constructed by Lanferman Associates in Francisco from earlier Mr. Lars, Incorporated sketches.

'Haskins,' Lars said.

'Pardon?' The KACH-man said.

'It's Colonel Haskins. Do you know,' he said meditatively to Henry Morris, 'that Nitz has fairly regularly avoided having anything to do with me, lately? Have you noted that puny bit of fact?'

Morris said, 'I note everything, Lars. Yes, it's in my death-rattle file.' Death-rattle ... the fireproof, Third-World-War proof, Titanian bolecricket-proof, well-hidden file-cases which were rigged to detonate in the event of Morris' death. He carried on his person a triggering mechanism sensitive to his heartbeat. Even Lars did not know where the files currently existed; probably in a hollow lacquered ceramic owl made from the guidance-system of item 207 in Morris's girl-friend's boy-friend's bathroom. And they contained all the originals of all the weapons-sketches which had ever emanated from Mr. Lars, Incorporated.

'What does it mean?' Lars asked.

'It means,' Morris said, protruding his lower jaw and waggling it, as if expecting it to come off, 'that General Nitz despises you.'

Taken aback, Lars said, 'Because of that one sketch? Two-oh-something, that p-thermotropic virus equipped to survive in dead space for a period greater than —'

'Oh no.' Morris shook his head vigorously. 'Because you're fooling yourself and him. Only he isn't fooled any more. In contrast to you.'

'How?'

Morris said, 'I hate to say it in front of all these people.'

'Go on and say it!' Lars said. But he felt sick. I really fear the Board, he realized. 'Client?' Is that what they are to me? *Boss*; that's the realistic word. UN-W Natsec groomed me, found me and built me up over the years, to replace Mr. Wade. I was there. I was ready and waiting eagerly when Wade Sokolarian died. And this knowledge that I have of *someone else waiting right now*, prepared for the day when I suffer cardiac arrest or experience the malfunction, the loss, of some other vital organ, waiting, too, in case I become *difficult —*

And, he thought, I am already difficult.

'Packard,' he said to the KACH-man, 'you're an independent organization. You operate anywhere in the world. Theoretically anyone can employ you.'

'Theoretically,' Packard agreed. 'You mean KACH itself, not me personally. I'm hired.'

16

'I thought you wanted to hear why General Nitz despises you,' Henry Morris said.

'No,' Lars said. 'Keep it to yourself.' I'll hire someone from KACH, a real pro, he decided, to scan UN-W, the whole apparatus if necessary, to find out what they're really up to regarding me. Especially, he thought, the success to which their next weapons medium has been brought; that's the crucial region for me to have exact knowledge about.

I wonder what they'd do, he thought, if they knew that it had so often occurred to me that I always could go over to Peep-East. If they, to insure their own safety, to shore up their absolute position of authority, tried to replace me —

He tried to imagine the size, shape and color of someone following him imprinting his own footsteps in his tracks. Child or youth, old woman or plump middle-aged man ... Wes-block psychiatrists, yoked to the state as servants, undoubtedly could turn up the psionic talent of contacting the Other World, the hyper-dimensional universe that he entered into during his trance-states. Wade had had it. Lilo Topchev had it. *He* had lots of it. So undoubtedly it existed elsewhere. And the longer he stayed in office the longer the Board had to ferret it out.

'May I say one thing,' Morris said, deferentially.

'Okay.' He waited, setting himself.

'General Nitz knew something was wrong when you turned down that honorary colonelcy in the UN-West Armed Forces.'

Staring at him, Lars said, 'But that was a gag! Just a piece of paper.'

'No,' Morris said. 'And you knew better – know better right now. Unconsciously, on an intuitive level. It would have made you legally subject to military jurisdiction.'

To no one in particular, the KACH-man said, 'It's true. They've called up virtually everyone they sent those gratis commissions to. Put them in uniform.' His face had become professionally impassive.

'God!' Lars felt himself cringe. It had been merely a whim, declining the honorary commission. He had given a gag answer to a gag document. And yet, now, on closer inspection —

'Am I right?' Henry Morris asked him, scrutinizing him.

'Yes,' Lars said, after a pause. 'I knew it.' He gestured. 'Well, the hell with it.' He turned his attention back to the KACH-collected weapons sketches. Anyhow, it was deeper than that; his troubles with UN-W Natsec went back farther and penetrated further than any inane scheme such as honorary commissions which all at once became the basis of mandatory military subjugation. What he objected to lay in an area where written documents did not exist. An area, in fact, which he did not care to think about.

Examining Miss Topchev's sketches he found himself confronted by this repellent aspect of his work – the lives of all of them, the Board included.

Here it was. And not by accident. It pervaded each design; he leafed among them and then tossed them back on his desk.

To the KACH-man he said, 'Weapons! Take them back; put them in your envelope.' There was not one weapon among them.

'As regards the concomodies —' Henry Morris began.

'What,' Lars said to him, 'is a concomody?'

Morris, taken aback, said, 'What do you mean, "What is a concomody?" You know. You sit down with them twice a month.' He gestured in irritation. 'You know more about the six concomodies on the Board than anyone else in Wes-bloc. Let's face it, everything you do is for them.'

'I'm facing it,' Lars said calmly. He folded his arms, sat back. 'But suppose when that TV autonomic interviewer out there asked me whether I was receiving something really spectacular I told it the truth.'

There was silence and then the KACH-man stirred and said. 'That's why they'd like you in uniform. You wouldn't be facing any TV cameras. There wouldn't be any opportunity for something to go wrong.' He left the sketches where they were on Lars' desk.

'Maybe it's already gone wrong,' Morris said, still studying his boss.

'No,' Lars said, presently. 'If it had you'd know.' Where Mr. Lars, Incorporated, stands, he thought, there'd just be a hole. Neat, precise, without a disturbance in the process to the adjoining high-rise structures. And achieved in roughly six seconds.

'I think you're nuts,' Morris decided. 'You're sitting here at your desk day after day, looking at Lilo's sketches, going quietly nuts. Every time you go into a trance a piece of you falls out.' His tone was harsh. 'It's too costly to you. And the upshot will be that one day a TV interviewer will nab you and say, "What's cooking, Mr. Lars, sir?" and you'll say something you shouldn't.' Dr. Todt, Elvira Funt, the KACH-man, all of them watched him with dismay but no one did or said anything. At his desk Lars stonily regarded the far wall and the Utrillo original which Maren Faine had given him at Christmas, 2003.

'Let's talk about something else,' Lars said. 'Where no pain's attached.' He nodded to Dr. Todt, who seemed more narrow and priest-like than ever. 'I think I'm psychologically ready now, doctor. We can instigate the autism, if you have your gadgets and you know what else set up.' Autism – a noble reference, dignified.

'I want an EEG first,' Dr. Todt said. 'Just as a safety factor.' He rolled the portable EEG machine forward. The preliminaries to the day's trance-state in which he lost contact with the given, shared universe, the *koinos kosmos*, and involvement in that other, mystifying realm, apparently an *idios kosmos*, a purely private world, began. But a purely private world in which a *aisthesis koine*, a common Something, dwelt.

What a way, Lars thought, to earn a living.

THREE

Greetings! said the letter, delivered by 'stant mail. You have been selected out of millions of your friends and neighbors.

You are now a concomody.

It can't be, Surley G. Febbs thought as he reread the printed form. It was a meager document, sizewise, with his name and number Xeroxed in. It looked no more serious than a bill from his conapt building's utility committee asking him to vote on a rate-increase. And yet here it was in his possession, formal evidence which would admit him, incredibly, into Festung, Washington, D.C. and its subsurface *kremlin*, the most heavily guarded spot in Wes-bloc.

And not as a tourist.

They found me typical! he said to himself. Just thinking this he *felt* typical. He felt swell and powerful and slightly drunk, and he had difficulty standing. His legs wobbled and he walked unsteadily across his miniature living-room and seated himself on his Ionian fnoolfur (imitation) couch.

'But I really know why they picked me,' Febbs said aloud. 'It's because I know all about weapons.' An authority; that's what he was, due to all the hours – six or seven a night, because like everyone else his work had been recently cut from twenty to nineteen hours per week – that he spent scanning edutapes at the Boise, Idaho main branch of the public library.

And not only an authority on weapons. He could remember with absolute clarity every fact he had ever learned – as for example on the manufacture of red stained glass in France during the early thirteenth century. I know the exact part of the Byzantine Empire from which the mosaics of the Roman period which they melted down to form the cherished red glass came, he said to himself, and exulted. It was about time that someone with universal knowledge like himself got on the UN-

W Natsec Board instead of the usual morons, the mass pursaps who read nothing but the headlines of the homeopapes and naturally the sports and animated cartoon strips and of course the dirty stuff about sex, and otherwise poisoned their empty minds with toxic, mass-produced garbage which was deliberately produced by the large corporations who really ran things, if you knew the inside story – as for instance I. G. Farben. Not to mention the much bigger electronics, guidance-systems and rocket trusts that evolved later, like A. G. Beimler of Bremen who really owned General Dynamics and I.B.M. and G.E., if you happened to have looked deeply into it. As he had.

Wait'll I sit down at the Board across from Commander-in-Chief Supreme UN-West General George Nitz, he said to himself.

I'll bet, he thought, I can tell him more facts about the hardware in the, for instance, Metro-gretel homeostatic anti-entrope phase-converter sine-wave oscillator that Boeing is using in their LL-40 peak-velocity interplan rocket than all the so-called 'experts' in Festung, Washington.

I mean, I won't be just replacing the concomody whose time on the Board expired and so I got this form. If I can get those fatheads to listen, I can replace entire bureaus.

This certainly beat sending letters to the Boise *Star-Times* 'pape and to Senator Edgewell, who didn't even respond with a form-letter any more, he was so, quote, busy. In fact this beat even the halcyon days, seven years ago, when due to the inheritance of a few UN-West gov bonds he had published his own small fact-sheet type of newsletter, which he had 'stant-mailed out at random to people in the vidphone book, plus of course to every government official in Washington. That had – or might well have had, if there weren't so many lardheads, Commies and bureaucrats in power – altered history ... for example in the area of cleaning up the importation of disease-causing protein molecules which regularly rode to Earth on ships returning from the colony planets, and which accounted for the flu that he, Febbs, had contracted in '99 and really never recovered from – as he had told the health-insurance official at his place of business, the New Era of Cooperative-Financing Savings & Loan Corporation of Boise, where Febbs examined applications for loans with an eye to detecting potential deadbeats.

In detecting deadbeats he was unmatched. He could look an applicant, especially a Negro, over in less than one microsecond and discern the actual composition of their ethical psychic-structure.

Which everyone at NECFS&LC knew, including Mr. Rumford, the branch manager. Although due to his egocentric personal ambitions and greed Mr. Rumford had deliberately sabotaged Febbs' repeated formal requests, over the last twelve years, for a more than routinely stipulated pay raise.

Now that problem was over. As a concomody he would receive a huge wage. He recalled, and felt momentary embarrassment, that often he had in his letters to Senator Edgewell among many other things complained about the salaries which the six citizens drafted onto the Board as concomodies received.

So now to the vidphone, to ring up Rumford, who was still at his high-rise conapt probably eating breakfast, and tell him to stuff it.

Febbs dialed and shortly found himself facing Mr. Rumford who still wore his Hong Kong-made silk bathrobe.

Taking a deep breath, Surley G. Febbs uttered, 'Mr. Rumford, I just wanted to tell you —'

He broke off, intimidated. Old habits die slowly. 'I got a notice from the UN-W Natsec people in Washington,' he heard his voice declare, thin and unsteady. 'So, um, you can g-get someone else t-to do all your d-dirty type jobs for you. And just in case you're interested, I let around six months ago a really bad apple take out a ten-thousand poscred loan, and he'll n-never pay it back.'

He then slammed the receiver down, perspiring, but weak with the wholesome joy that now lodged everywhere inside him.

And I'm not going to tell you *who* that bad apple is, he said to himself. You can comb the minned mass of records on your own time, pay my replacement to do it. Up yours, Mr Rumford.

Going into the tiny kitchen of his conapt he quick-unfroze a pack of stewed apricots, his customary breakfast. Seated at the table which extended, plank-like from the wall, he ate and meditated.

Wait until the Organization hears about this, he reflected. By this he meant the Superior Warriors of Caucasian Ancestry of Idaho and Oregon, Chapter Fifteen. Especially Roman Centurion Skeeter W. Johnstone, who just recently by means of an aa-35 disciplinary edict had demoted Febbs from the rank of Legionnaire Class One to Helot Class Fifty.

I'll be hearing from the Organization's Praetorian Headquarters at Cheyenne, he realized. From Emperor-of-the-Sun Klaus himself! They'll want to make *me* an R.C. – and probably kick out Johnstone on his tail.

There were a lot of others who would get what they deserved now. For instance that thin librarian at the main branch of the Boise publibe who had denied him access to the eight closed cases of microtapes of all the twentieth century pornographic novels. This means your job, he said to himself, and imagined the expression on her dried, wart-like face as she received the news from General Nitz himself.

As he ate his stewed apricots, he pictured in his mind the great bank of computers at Festung, Washington, D.C. as they had examined million after million of file cards and all the data on them, determining who was *really* typical in his buying habits and who was only faking it, like the Strattons in the conapt across from his who always tried to appear typical but who in no true ontological sense made it.

I mean, Febbs thought joyfully, I'm Aristotle's Universal Man, such as society has tried to breed genetically for five thousand years! And Univox-50R at Festung, Washington, finally recognized it!

When a weapon-component is at last put before me officially, he thought with grim assurance, I'll know how to plowshare it, all right. They can count on me. I'll come up with a dozen ways to plowshare it, and all of them good. Based on my knowledge and skill.

What's odd is that they'd still need the other five con-comodies. Maybe they'll realize that. Maybe instead of giving me only a one-sixth slice they'll give me all the components. They might as well.

It would go about like this:

General Nitz (amazed): Good God, Febbs! You're com-pletely right. This stage one of the Brownian movement-restriction field-induction coil, portable subtype, can be easily plowshared into an inexpensive source to chill beer on excur-sions lasting over seven hours. Whew! Gollee!

Febbs: However I think you're still missing the basic point, General. If you'll look more closely at my official abstract on the —

The vidphone rang, then, interrupting his thoughts; he rose from the breakfast table, hurried to answer it.

On the screen a middle-aged female Wes-bloc bureaucrat appeared. 'Mr. Surley G. Febbs of Conapt Building 300685?'

'Yes,' he said, nervously.

'You received your notice by 'stant mail of your induction as concomody to the UN-W Natsec Board as of this following Tuesday.'

'Yes!'

'I am calling, Mr. Febbs, to remind you that under no cir-cumstances are you to convey, reveal, expound, announce or otherwise inform any person or organization or info-media or autonomic extension thereof capable of receiving, recording and/or transmitting, communicating and/or telecasting data in any form whatsoever, that you have been legally named by due and official process to the UN-W Natsec Board as Con-comody A, as per paragraph III in your written notice, which you are required under penalty of law to read and strictly observe.'

Surley Febbs, inside himself, fainted dead away. He had failed to read all the way down the notice. Of course the iden-tity of the six concomodies on the Board was a matter of strict secrecy! And already he had told Mr. Rumford.

Or had he? Frantically, he tried to recall his exact words.

Hadn't he merely said he received a notice? Oh God. If they found out —

'Thank you, Mr. Febbs,' the female official said, and rang off. Febbs stood in silence, gradually hinging himself back together.

I'll have to call Mr. Rumford again, he realized. Make certain he thinks I'm quitting for health reasons. Some pretext. I've lost my conapt, have to leave the area. Anything!

He found himself shaking.

A new scene bloomed frighteningly in his mind.

General Nitz (grayly, with menace): So you told, Febbs.

Febbs: You need me, General. You really do! I can plow-share better than anyone drafted before – Univox-50R knows what it's talking about. In the name of God, sir! Give me a chance to prove my superior worth.

General Nitz (moved): Well, all right, Febbs. I can see you're not quite like anyone else. We can afford to treat you differently, because the fact is that in all my long years of dealing with all kinds of people I have never seen anyone as unique as you and it would be a distinct loss to the Free World if you decided not to stick with us and give us the benefit of your knowledge, experience and talent.

Reseating himself at his breakfast table, Febbs mechanically resumed the eating which had been interrupted.

General Nitz: Actually, Febbs, I'd even go so far as to say —

Aw, the hell with it, Febbs thought with growing, overwhelming gloom.

FOUR

Toward noon the ranking engineer from Lanferman Associates of San Francisco and Los Angeles, the firm which produced the mockups and prototypes and whatnot from Lars Powderdry's sketches, showed up at the New York office of Mr. Lars, Incorporated.

Pete Freid, at home here from long years of experience, sauntered round-shouldered and stooped but still tall into Lars' office. He found Lars drinking a solution of honey and synthetic amino acids in a twenty per cent alcohol base: an antidote to the depletion of body-constituents by the trance-state which had occurred earlier in the morning.

Pete said, 'They found that what you're swilling is one of the ten major causes of upper g.i. cancer. Better quit now.'

'I can't quit,' Lars said. His body needed the replacement-source and anyhow Peter was kidding. 'What I ought to quit —' he began and then became silent. Today he had talked too much already, and before the man from KACH, who, if he was any good, remembered, recorded and put on permanent file everything he heard.

Pete wandered about the office, crouched for all eternity from his excessive height and also, as he tirelessly reiterated, his 'bad back.' There was a certain vagueness as to what the bad back consisted of. Some days it was a slipped disk. Other times, according to Pete's rambling monologs, it was a worn disk; the distinction between these two eternal, Jobish afflictions he never ceased delineating. On Wednesdays, for example today, it was due to an old war-time injury. He dilated on that now.

'Sure,' he told Lars, his hands in the rear pockets of his work-trousers. He had flown three thousand miles from the West Coast aboard the public jet, wearing his grease-stained shop clothes, with, as a concession to human society, a twisted, now black but perhaps formerly brightly colored necktie. The tie hung like a lead-rope from his unbuttoned, sweaty shirt, as if, under former slave conditions, Pete had been led periodically to slaughter by means of it. Certainly he had not been led to pasture. Despite his rambling, ambulatory, psychomotor activity he was a born worker. Everything else in his life – his wife and three children, his hobbies, his friendships – these fell to ruin when work-time came. And for him this arrived at eye-opening time at six or six-thirty in the morning. He was, in contrast to what Lars regarded as neurologically normal humanity, a wide-awake early riser. It amounted to a defect. And this after a fugue the night before, until bar-closing time, of beer and pizza, with or without Molly, his wife.

'What do you mean, "sure"?' Lars said, sipping his special drink. He felt weary; today's trance-state had enervated him beyond the recall of the chemical elixir. 'Okay, you mean, "Sure, I ought to quit my job." I know the rubric you've got to offer. Frankly I've heard it so many times I could —'

Pete interrupted, in his agitated, husky, urgent voice, 'Aw, the hell you know what I mean. Bull! You never listen. All you do is go to heaven and come back with the word of God, and we're supposed to believe as gospel every stupid thing you write down, like some —' He gestured, tic-like, his big frame shuddering under his blue cotton shirt. 'Look at the service you could do humanity if you weren't so lazy.'

'What service?'

'You could solve all our problems!' Pete glowered at him. 'If they've got weapons designs up there —' He jerked his thumb vaguely toward the ceiling of the office, as if, during his trance-states, Lars literally rose. 'Science ought to investigate you. Chrissake, you ought to be at Cal Tech being examined, not running, this fairy outfit you run.'

'Fairy,' Lars said.

'Okay, maybe you're not a fairy. So what? My brother-in-law's a fairy and that's okay with me. A guy can be anything he wants.' Pete's voice rose to a shout that boomed and echoed. 'As long as it's integrity, it's what he really is and not what he's *told* to do. You!' His tone was withering, now. 'You do what they tell you. They say, Go get us a bunch of primary design-concepts in two-D form, and you do!'

He lowered his voice, grunted, rubbed his perspiring upper lip. Then, seating himself, he reached his long arms out, groping for the heap of sketches on Lars' desk.

'These aren't them,' Lars said, retaining the sketches.

'These aren't? Then what are they? They look like designs to me.' Pete twisted his head, extended his neck, piston-wise, to peer.

Lars said, 'From Peep-East. Miss Topchev's.' Pete's opposite number is Bulganingrad or New Moscow – the Soviets had two design-engineering firms available, the typical overlapping duplication of a monolithic society – had the task of rendering *these* to their next step.

'Can I see them?'

Lars passed them to Pete, who put his nose almost against the flat, glossy surfaces, as if suddenly near-sighted. He said nothing for a time as he turned from one to the next, and then he snarled, sat back, hurled the stack of pics onto the desk. Or nearly onto it. The stack fell to the floor.

Pete, stretching, picked them up, respectfully straightened them until they were precisely even, one with the next, and set them down on the desk, demonstrating that he had meant no incivility. 'They're terrible,' he said.

'No,' Lars said. No more so than his own, actually. Pete's loyalty to him, as a person, made a puppet out of Pete's jaws; friendship wagged the big man's tongue, and although Lars appreciated this he preferred to see the record set straight. 'They can go into plowshare. She's doing her job.' But of course these sketches might not be representative. The Soviets had a notorious reputation for managing to traduce KACH. The planet-wide police agency was fair game for the Soviets' own secret police, the KVB. It had not been discussed at the time Don Packard had produced the sketches, but the fact was just this: the Soviets, onto the presence of a KACH agent at their weapons fashion designs level, probably showed only what they cared to show, and held the rest back. That

28

always had to be assumed.

Or at least *he* assumed that. What UN-W Natsec did with *their* KACH-obtained material was something else; he had no knowledge of that. The Board's policy could range from total credulity (although that was hardly likely) to utter cynicism. He, himself, tried to seek out a moderate middle-ground.

Pete said, 'And that fuzzy print, that's her. Right?'

'Yes.' Lars showed him the blurred glossy.

Again Pete put his nose to the subject of his scrutiny. 'You can't tell anything,' he decided finally. 'And for this KACH gets money! I could do better just by walking into the Bulganingrad Institute for Defensive Implementation Research Division with a polaroid Land-camera.'

'There's no such place,' Lars said.

Pete glanced up. 'You mean they abolished their bureau? But she's still at her desk.'

'It's now under someone else, not Victor Kamow. He disappeared. A lung condition. It's now called —' Lars turned up the memo he had taken from the KACH-man's report. In Peep-East this happened continually; he attached no importance to it – 'Minor Protocides, Subdivision Crop-production, Archives. Of Bulganingrad. A branch of Middle Auton-tool Safety Standards Ministry, which is their cover for their non-bacteriological warfare research agencies of every kind. As you know.' He bumped heads with Pete, inspecting the fuzzy glossy-print of Lilo Topchev, as if time alone might have brought from the blur a more accessible image.

'What is it,' Pete said, 'that obsesses you?'

Lars shrugged. 'Nothing. Divine discontent maybe.' He felt evasive; the engineer from Lanferman Associates was too keen an observer, too capable.

'No, I mean – but first —'

Pete expertly ran his sensitive, long, stained-dark fingers along the underside of Lars' desk, seeking a monitoring device. Finding none immediately at hand he continued. 'You're a scared man. Do you still take pills?'

'No.'

'You're lying.'

Lars nodded. 'I'm lying.'

'Sleeping bad?'

'Medium.'

'If that horse's ass Nitz has got your goat —'

'It's not Nitz. To reshuffle your picturesque language, that goat's horse Nitz has not got my ass. So are you satisfied? Sir?'

Pete said, 'They can groom replacements for you for fifty years and not come up with anyone like you. I knew Wade. He was okay but he wasn't in the same league as you. No one is. Especially not that dame in Bulganingrad.'

'It's nice of you,' Lars began, but Pete cut him savagely off.

'Nice – schnut! Anyhow, that's not it.'

'No,' Lars agreed. 'That's not it and don't insult Lilo Top-chev.'

Fumbling in his shirt pocket Pete brought out a cheap, drugstore-style cigar. He lit up, puffed its noxious fumes until the office dissolved and reeked. Oblivious, without giving a damn, Pete wheezed the smoke in and out, silent as he pondered.

He had this virtue/defect: anything puzzling, he believed, if worried at long enough, could be elucidated. In any area. Even that of the human psyche. The machine was no more and no less complicated, according to him, than biological organs created by two billions years of evolution.

It was, Lars thought, an almost childishly optimistic view; it dated from the eighteenth century. Pete Freid, for all his manual skills, his engineering genius, was an anachronism. He had the outlook of a bright seventh-grader.

'I've got kids,' Pete said, chewing on his cigar, making a bad thing worse. 'You need a family.'

'Sure,' Lars said.

'No, I'm not serious.'

'Of course you are. But that doesn't make you right. I know what's bothering me. Look.'

Lars touched the code-trips of his locked desk drawer. Responding to his fingertips the drawer at once, cash-register-like, shot open. From it he brought forth his own new sketches, the items which Pete had traveled three thousand miles to see. He passed them over, and felt the pervasive guilt which always accompanied this moment. His ears burned. He could not look directly at Pete. Instead he busied himself with his appointment gimmicks, anything to keep himself from thinking during this moment.

Pete said presently, 'These are swell.' He carefully initialed each sketch, beneath the official number which the UN-W Natsec bureaucrat had stamped, sealed and signed.

'You're going back to San Francisco,' Lars said, 'and you're going to whip up a poly-something model, then begin on a working prototype —'

'My boys are,' Pete corrected. 'I just tell them what to do. You think I get my hands dirty? With poly-something?'

Lars said, 'Pete, how the hell long can it go on?'

'Forever,' Pete said, promptly. The seventh-grader's combination of naïve optimism and an almost ferociously embittered resignation.

Lars said, 'This morning, before I could get inside the building, here, one of those autonomic TV interviewers from Lucky Bagman's show cornered me. They believe. *They actually believe.*'

'So they believe. That's what I mean.' Pete gestured agitatedly with his cheap cigar. 'Don't you get it? Even if you had looked that TV lens right in the eye, so to speak, and you had said calmly and clearly, maybe something like this: "You think I'm making weapons? You think, *that's* what I'm bringing back from hyper-space, from that niddy-noddy realm of the supernatural?"'

'But they need to be protected,' Lars said.

'Against what?'

'Against anything. Everything. They deserve protection; they think we're doing our job.'

After a pause Pete said, 'There's no protection in weapons. Not any more. Not since – you know. 1945. When they wiped out that Jap city.'

'But,' Lars said, 'the pursaps think there is. There *seems* to be.'

'And that *seems* to be what they're getting.'

Lars said, 'I think I'm sick. I'm involved in a delusional world. I ought to have been a pursap – without my talent as a medium I would be, I wouldn't know what I know; I wouldn't be on the inside looking out. I'd be one of those fans of Lucky Bagman and his morning TV interview show that accepts what he's told, knows it's true because he saw it on that big screen with all those stereo colors, richer than life. It's fine while I'm actually in the comatose state, in the damn trance; there I'm fully involved. Nothing off in a corner of my mind jeers.'

' "Jeers." What do you mean?' Pete eyed him anxiously.

'Doesn't something inside you jeer?' He was amazed.

'Hell no! Something inside me says, You're worth twice the poscreds they're paying you; *that's* what something inside *me* says, and it's right. I mean to take that up with Jack Lanferman one of these days.' Pete glared in self-righteous anger.

'I thought you felt the same way,' Lars said. And come to think of it, he had assumed that all of them, even General George McFarlane Nitz, stood in relationship to what they were doing as he stood: corrupted by shame, afflicted with the sense of guilt that made it impossible for him to meet anyone eye-to-eye.

'Let's go down to the corner and have a cup of coffee,' Pete said.

'It's time for a break.'

FIVE

The coffee house as an institution, Lars knew, had great historicity behind it. This one invention had cleared the cobwebs from the minds of the English intellectuals at the period of Samuel Johnson, had eradicated the fog inherited from the seventeenth century's pubs. The insidious stout, sack and ale had generated – not wisdom, sparkling wit, poetry or even political clarity – but muddied resentment, mutual and pervasive, that had degenerated into religious bigotry. That, and the pox, had decimated a great nation.

Coffee had reversed the trend. History had taken a decisive new turn . . . and all because of a few beans frozen in the snow which the defenders of Vienna had discovered after the Turks had withdrawn.

And here, already in a booth, cup in hand, sat small, pretty Miss Bedouin, with her pointed silver-tipped breasts fashionably in sight. She greeted him as he entered. 'Mr. Lars! Sit with me, okay?'

'Okay,' he said, and he and Pete shuffled and squeezed in on both sides of her.

Surveying Miss Bedouin, Pete interlaced his fingers and rested his hairy arms on the table of the booth. He said to her, 'Hey, how come you can't beat out that girl he keeps to run his Paris office, that Maren something?'

'Mr. Freid,' Miss Bedouin said, 'I'm not sexually interested in anyone.'

Grinning, Pete glanced at Lars. 'She's candid.'

Candor, Lars thought, at Mr. Lars, Incorporated. Ironic! A waste. But then Miss Bedouin didn't know what went on. She was sublimely pursap. As if the era before the Fall had been re-established for roughly four billion citizens of Wes-bloc and Peep-East. The burden, which had once been everyone's rested now on the cogs alone. The cognoscenti had relieved their race of a curse ... if 'cog' really derived from that and not, as he suspected, from an English rather than Italian word.

The English archaic definition had always seemed almost supernaturally apt to him. Cog. Using one's finger as a sort of cog to guide or hold the dice; i.e. to cozen, wheedle; to cheat.

But I could be candid, too, he thought, if I didn't know anything; I see no particular merit in that. Since medieval times a fool – no offense to you, Miss Bedouin – has been permitted the liberty of wagging his tongue. But suppose, just for this one moment, as we sit pressed together in this booth, the three of us, two cog males and one dainty silver-tipped pursap girl whose cardinal preoccupation resides in a perpetual concern that her admittedly lovely little pointed breasts be as conspicuous as possible ... suppose I could cheerfully pass back and forth as you do, without the need to sharply split what I know from what I say.

The wound would be healed, he decided. No more pills. No more nights of being unable – or unwilling – to sleep.

'Miss Bedouin,' he said, 'I actually am in love with you. But don't misunderstand. I'm talking about a spiritual love. Not carnal.'

'Okay,' Miss Bedouin said.

'Because,' Lars said, 'I admire you.'

'You admire her so much,' Pete said grumbling, 'that you can't go to bed with her? Kid stuff! How old are you, Lars? Real love means going to bed, like in marriage. Aren't I right, Miss whatever-your-name is? If Lars really loved you —'

'Let me explain,' Lars said.

'Nobody wants to hear your explanation,' Pete said.

'Give me a chance,' Lars said. 'I admire her position.'

' "Not so perpendicular," ' Pete said, quoting the great old-time composer and poet of the last century, Marc Blitzstein.

Flaring up, Miss Bedouin said, 'I am *too* perpendicular. That's what I just now told you. And not only that —'

She ceased, because a small, elderly man with the final glimmerings of white hairs coating irregularly a pinkish, almost glowing scalp, had abruptly appeared by their booth. He wore ancient lens-glasses, carried a briefcase, and his manner was a mixture of timidity and determination, as if he could not turn back now, but would have liked to.

Pete said, 'A salesman.'

'No,' Miss Bedouin said. 'Not well dressed enough.'

'Process-server,' Lars said; the elderly, short gentleman had an official look to him. 'Am I right?' he asked.

The elderly gentleman said haltingly, 'Mr. Lars?'

'That's me,' Lars said; evidently his guess had been correct.

'Autograph collector,' Miss Bedouin said, in triumph. 'He wants your autograph, Mr. Lars; he recognizes you.'

'He's not a bum,' Pete added reflectively. 'Look at that stickpin in his tie. That's a real cut stone. But who today wears —'

'Mr. Lars,' the elderly gentleman said, and managed to seat himself precariously at the rim of the booth. He laid his brief-case before him, clearing aside the sugar, salt and empty coffee cups. 'Forgive me that I am bothering you. But – a problem.' His voice was low, frail. He had about him a Santa Claus quality, and yet he had come on business, something firmer and without sentiment. He employed no elves and he was not here to give away toys. He was an expert: it showed in the way he rooted in his briefcase.

All at once Pete nudged Lars and pointed. Lars saw, at an empty booth near the door, two younger men with vapid, cod-like, underwater faces; they had entered along with this odd fellow and were keeping an eye on matters.

At once Lars reached into his coat, whipped out the docu-ment he carried constantly with him. To Miss Bedouin he said, 'Call a cop.'

She blinked, half-rose to her feet.

'Go on,' Pete said roughly to her; then, raising his voice, said loudly, 'Somebody get a cop!'

'Please,' the elderly gentleman said, pleadingly but with a trace of annoyance. 'Just a few words. There's something we don't understand.' He now had in sight pics, glossy color shots which Lars recognized. These consisted of KACH-accumu-lated reproductions of his own earlier sketches, the 260 through 265 sequence, plus shots of final accurate specs drawn up for presentation to Lanferman Associates.

Lars, unfolding his document, said to the elderly man, 'This is a writ of restraint. You know what it says?'

Distastefully, with reluctance, the elderly man nodded.

'Any and every official of the Government of the Soviet Union,' Lars said, 'of Peoples' China, Cuba, Brazil, the Dominican Republic, —'

'Yes, yes,' the elderly gentleman agreed, nodding.

'"— and all other ethnic or national entities comprising the political entity Peep-East, is restrained and enjoined during the pendency of this action from harassing, annoying, molesting, threatening or striking the plaintiff – myself, Lars Powderdry – or in any manner occupying him or being upon or within proximity so that —"'

'Okay,' the elderly gentleman said. 'I am a Soviet official. Legally I cannot talk to you; we know that, Mr. Lars. But this sketch, your number 265. See?' He turned the KACH-manufactured glossy for Lars to examine; Lars ignored it. 'Someone in your staff wrote on this that it is —' the wrinkled, plump finger traced the English words at the foot of the sketch – 'is "Evolution Gun." Correct?'

Pete said loudly, 'Yes, and watch out or it'll turn you back into protoplasmic slime.'

'No, not the trance-sketch,' the Soviet official said, and chuckled slyly. 'Must have prototype. You are from Lanferman Associates? You make up the model and prove-test? Yes, I think you are. I am Aksel Kaminsky.' He held out his hand to Pete. 'You are —?'

A New York City patrol ship flopped to the pavement before the coffee shop. Two uniformed policemen hastened, hand at holster, through the doorway with glances that took in everyone, anything or person capable of harm, activity and/or motion – and most particularly those who might be able to in any fashion, wise or manner whatsoever draw a weapon of their own.

'Over here,' Lars said, heavily. He disliked this, but the Soviet authorities were behaving idiotically. How could they expect to approach him like this, openly, in a public place? Rising, he held his restraining writ out to the first of the two-man team of police.

'This person,' he said, indicating the elderly Peep-East official who sat frowning, drumming nervously with his fingers against his briefcase, 'is in contempt of the Superior Court of Queens County, Department Three. I'd like him arrested. My attorney will ask that charges be pressed. I'm supposed to tell you that,' he said. He waited while the two policemen studied the writ.

'All I want to know,' the elderly Soviet official said plaintively, 'is part 76, your number. What does it refer to?'

He was led off. At the doorway the two silent ultra-neat, fashionable, cod-eyed young men who had accompanied him pursued his retreating figure but made no move to interfere with the actions of the city police. They were unemotional and resigned.

'All in all,' Pete said presently as he sat down again, 'it wasn't too messy.' He grimaced, however. Clearly he hadn't enjoyed it. 'Ten will get you twenty he's from the embassy.'

'Yes,' Lars agreed. Undoubtedly from the USSR Embassy, rather than the SeRKeb. He had been given instructions and had sought only to carry them out, to satisfy his superiors. They were all on that ratwheel. The encounter hadn't been pleasant to the Soviets, either.

'Funny they were so interested in 265,' Pete said. 'We haven't had any trouble with it. Who do you suppose on your staff is working for KACH? Is it worth having the FBI check them over?'

'There isn't a chance in the world,' Lars said, 'that the FBI or CIA or anybody else in the business could pry loose the KACH-man on our staff. You know that. What about the one at Lanferman Associates? I saw shots of your mockups.' He had of course known that anyhow. What bothered him was not the verification that KACH had someone at Mr. Lars, Incorporated – that Peep-East knew as much about his output as he did about Miss Topchev's – but that something ailed item 265. Because he had favored that. He had followed it through

37

its several stages with interest. The prototype, down in Lanferman's almost endless subsurface chambers, was being tested this week.

Tested, anyhow, in one sense.

But if he let himself dwell on that long enough, he would have to abandon his profession. He did not blame Jack Lanferman and certainly not Pete. Neither of them made the rules or defined the game. Like himself they sat passive, because this was the law of life.

And in the subsurface chambers that linked Lanferman Associates of San Francisco with their 'branch' in Los Angeles – actually merely the south end of the titanic underground network of the organization itself – item 265, the Evolution Gun (a hastily scrawled screed of a title, in the trade deprived of durability by adding the term *working* to it), this superweapon snatched from the puzzling realm which the weapons-mediums groped about in, would see what the pursaps liked to think of as – action.

Some ersatz gross victim, susceptible of being expanded, would be treated to a swat from item 265. And all this would be caught by the lenses of the media, the mags, the books, the 'papes, the TV, everything except helium-filled blimps towing red neon signs.

Yes, Lars thought; Wes-bloc could add that to its repertory of media by which the pursaps are kept both pure and saps. Something that lights up ought to cross the nighttime sky very slowly, or, as in former times, sputter unendingly around and around the turret of a skyscraper, edifying the public to the extent desired. Due to the highly specialized nature of this info-medium, it would have to be phrased simply, of course.

The blimp could initiate its journey, Lars reflected, with what might be a sanguine piece of knowledge. That the 'action' which item 265 was now seeing beneath the surface of California was utterly faked.

It would not be appreciated. The pursaps would be furious. Not UN-W Natsec, he realized. They could take such a leak in their stride. The cogs would survive an exposure of that and every other datum their possession of which defined them as a ruling elite. No, it would be the pursaps who would crumble. And that was the part that made him feel the impotent anger that eroded, day by day, his sense of his own worth and the worth of his work.

Right here in this coffee shop, Joe's Sup & Sip, he realized, I could stand up and yell, *There are no weapons*. And I'd get – a few pale, frightened faces. And then the pursaps within range would scatter, get out as fast as possible.

I know this. Aksel Kandinsky or Kaminsky or whatever it calls itself, the kindly, elderly official from the Soviet Embassy – he knows. Pete knows. General Nitz and his kind know.

Item 265 is as successful as anything I have ever produced and ever will produce, the Evolution Gun which should turn every living sentient, highly organized life form within a five-mile radius back two billion years, devolved to the most remote past; articulated morphological structures should give way to something resembling an amoeba, a slime lacking a spine, fins; something unicellular, on the order of a filterable protein molecule. And this the audience of pursaps watching the six o'clock news-roundup on TV, will see, because it will happen. In a sense.

In that, fake heaped on fake, it will be staged before the variety of cameras. And the pursaps can go to bed happy, knowing that their lives and the lives of their kids are protected by Thor's hammer from The Enemy; that is, from Peep-East, which is also mightily testing their disaster-producing tearweps of havoc.

God would be amazed, probably pleased, by the ruin items 260 through 280, when built by Lanferman Associates, can call into being. It is the Greek sin of *hubris* made incarnate logos-wise in the flesh – or rather in polysomething and metal, miniaturized with backup systems throughout in case some gnat-sized component fails.

And even God, in raring back and passing the original miracle, The Creation, hadn't gone into miniaturized backup system. He had put all His eggs in one faultily woven basket, the sentient race which now photographed in 3-D ultra-stereophonic, videomatic depth something which did not exist. He thought, don't knock it until you've tried it. Because getting clear 3-D ultra-stereophonic, videomatic depth shots of constructs which do not exist is not easy. It has taken us fifteen thousand years.

Aloud he said, 'The priests of ancient Egypt. Circa Herodotus.'

'Pardon?' Pete said.

Lars said, 'They used hydraulic pressure to open temple doors at a distance. As they raised their arms and prayed to the animal-headed gods.'

'I don't get it,' Pete said.

'You don't see?' Lars said, feeling baffled. It was so obvious to him. 'It's a monopoly, Pete. That's what we've got, a goddam monopoly. That's the whole point.'

'You've gone nuts,' Pete said grumpily. He fooled with the handle of his empty coffee cup. 'Don't let that Peep-East flunky come in here and get you shook.'

'It's not him.' Lars wanted to make his point; he felt the urgency of it. 'Down below Monterey,' he said, 'where nobody can see. Where you fellas run the prototypes. Cities blown up, satellites knocked down ' He halted, Pete was jerking his head warningly toward silver-tipped Miss Bedouin. 'A hedgehog satellite,' Lars said carefully, thinking of the most ominous extant. The hedgehogs were considered impenetrable, and out of the more than seven hundred Earth-satellites in current orbit, almost fifty were hedgehogs. 'Items 221,' he said. 'The Ionizing Fish that decomposed to the molecular level, drifted as gas —'

'Shut up,' Pete said harshly.

They finished their coffee in silence.

SIX

That evening Lars Powderdry met his mistress Maren Faine at the Paris branch of Mr. Lars, Incorporated, where Maren maintained an office as elaborate as —

He searched for the metaphor, but Maren's esthetic tastes eluded description. Hands in his pockets he gazed around him as Maren disappeared into the powder room to make ready for the real world. For her, existence began when the workday ended. And this despite the fact of her high managerial position. Logically she should have been career-oriented, as involved in her vocation as the darkest, most sullen Calvinist.

But it had not worked out that way. Maren was twenty-nine, slightly tall – she stood five-seven barefoot – with luminous red hair. No, not red; it was mahogany in tone, polished, not like the artificial, photograph-grained plastic but the real thing. Yes, Maren's coloration had been proved authentic. She woke up illuminated, eyes bright as – hell, he thought. What did it matter? Who cared at seven-thirty in the morning? A beautiful, alert, slightly-too-tall woman, colorful and graceful and muscular at that time of day, was an offense to reason and an abomination to sexuality, in that what did one do with her? At least after the first few weeks. One could hardly go on and on ...

As Maren re-entered the office, coat over her shoulders, he said. 'You really don't care what goes on here.'

'You mean the enterprise? The incorporated?' Her cat-eyes flew wide, merrily; she was way ahead of him. 'Look, you have my *soma* at night and my mind all day long. What else do you want?'

Lars said, 'I hate education. I'm not kidding. *Soma*. Where'd you learn that?' He felt hungry, irritable, at loose ends. Due to the buggery of contemporary time-zone computation he had in actuality been on his feet sixteen hours.

'You hate me,' Maren said, in the tone of a marriage counselor. I know your *real* motivations, the tone implied. And it also implied: And you don't.

Maren gazed at him squarely, unafraid of anything he might do or say. He reflected that although technically he could fire her by day, or kick her out of his Paris conapt by night, he had really no hold over her. Whether her career meant anything to her or not, she could get a good job anywhere. Any time. She did not need him. If they parted company she would miss him for a week or so, grieve to the extent of bawling unexpectedly after the third martini ... but that would be it.

On the other hand, if he were to lose her the wound would never close.

'Want dinner?' he said unenthusiastically.

Maren said, 'No. Want prayer.'

He stared at her. 'W-what?'

Calmly she said, 'I want to go to church and light a candle and pray. What's so strange about that? I do it a couple of times a week, you know that. You knew it when you first —' Delicately she finished, '*Knew* me. In the Biblical sense. I told you that first night.'

'Candle for what?' Lighting a candle had to be *for* something.

Maren said, 'My secret.'

Feeling baffled he said, 'I'm going to bed. It may be six o'clock to you but it's past two a.m. for me. Let's go to your conapt and you can fix me something light to eat and then I'll get some sleep and you can go pray.' He started toward the door.

'I heard,' Maren said, 'that a Soviet official managed to get to you today.'

That startled him. 'Where'd you hear that?'

'I got a warning. From the Board. An official reprimand to the firm, telling us to beware of short old men.'

'I doubt it.'

Maren shrugged. 'The Paris office ought to be informed, don't you agree? It did happen in a public place.'

42

'I didn't seek the idiot out! He approached me – I was just having a cup of coffee.' But he felt uneasy. Had the Board really transmitted an official reprimand? If so, it ought to have come to his attention.

'That general,' Maren said, 'whose name I always forget – the fat one you're so afraid of. Nitz.' She smiled; the spear in his side twisted. 'General Nitz contacted us here in Paris via the ultra-closed-circuit vidline and he said to be more careful. I said talk to you. He said —'

'You're making this up.' But he could see she wasn't. Probably it had happened within the hour of his meeting with Aksel Kaminsky. Maren had had all day to relay General Nitz's warning to him. It was like her to wait until now, when his blood-sugar was low and he had no defense. 'I better call him,' he said, half to himself.

'He's in bed. Consult the time-zone chart for Portland, Oregon. Anyhow I explained it all to him.' She walked out into the hall and he followed, reflexively; together they waited for the elevator which would carry them to the roof field where his hopper, property of the firm, was parked. Maren hummed happily to herself, maddening him.

'You explained it how?'

'I said you had been considering for a long time that in case you weren't liked, appreciated here, you intended to 'coat.'

Levelly, he said, 'And what was his answer?'

'General Nitz said yes, he realized that you could always 'coat. He appreciated your position. In fact the military on the Board, at their special closed session at Festung, Washington, D.C. last Wednesday had discussed this. And General Nitz's staff reported that they had three more weapons fashion designers standing by. Three new mediums which that psychiatrist at the Wallingford Clinic at St. George, Utah had turned up.'

'Is this on the level?'

'Sort of.'

He made a quick computation. 'It's not two a.m. in Oregon; it's noon. High noon.' Turning, he started back toward her office.

'You're forgetting,' Maren said, 'that we're now on Toliver Econ-time time.'

'But in Oregon the sun's in the middle of the sky!'

Patiently, Maren said, 'But still by T.E.T. it's two a.m. Don't call General Nitz; give up. If he had wanted to talk to you he would have called the New York office, not here. He doesn't *like* you; that's what it is, midnight or midday.' She smiled pleasantly.

Lars said, 'You're sowing seeds of discontent.'

'Truth-telling,' she disagreed. 'W.t.k.w.y.t.i.?'

'No,' he said. 'I don't want to know what my trouble is.'

'Your trouble —'

'*Lay, off.*'

Maren continued, 'Your trouble is that you feel uneasy when you have to deal with myths, or as you would put it, lies. So all day long you go around uneasy. But then when someone starts talking the truth you break out in a rash; you get psychosomatically ill from head to toe.'

'Hmm.'

'The answer,' Maren said, 'at least from the standpoint of those who have to deal with you, temperamental and mercurial as you are, is to tell you the myth —'

'Oh, shut up. Did Nitz give any details about these new mediums they'd uncovered?'

'Sure. One small boy, as fat as Tweedledee, sucking a lollypop, very disagreeable. One middle-aged spinster lady in Nebraska. One —'

'Myths,' Lars said. 'Told so they seem true.'

He strode back up the corridor to Maren's office. A moment later he was unlocking her vidset; dialing Festung, Washington, D.C. and the Board's mundane stations.

But as the picture formed he heard a sharp click. The picture minutely — but perceptibly, if you looked closely enough — shrank. And at the same time a red warning light lit up.

The vidset was tapped somewhere along its transmitting cable. And not by a mere coil but by a splice-in. At once he rang off, got to his feet, rejoined Maren, who had let one elevator go by and was serenely waiting for him.

44

'Your set's tapped.'

'I know,' Maren said.

'And you haven't called PT&T to come in and remove the tap?'

Maren said graciously, as if talking to someone with severe intellectual limitations, 'Look, they know anyhow.' A vague-enough reference: *they*. Either KACH, the disinterested agency, hired by Peep-East, or extensions of Peep-East itself such as its KVB. As she as much as said, it didn't matter. *They* knew it all anyhow.

Still, it annoyed him, trying to reach his client through a conduit tapped in such a way that no effort, not even the for-mality, had been made to conceal the introduction of a hostile, self-serving, highly unnatural bit of electronic mechanism.

Maren said thoughtfully, 'It was put on last week some-time.'

Lars said, 'I do not object to a monopoly of knowledge by one small class. It doesn't upset me, that there are a few cogs and a lot of pursaps. Every society is really run by an elite.'

'So what's the trouble, darling dear?'

'What bothers me,' Lars said as the up-elevator came and he and Maren entered it, 'is that the elite, in this case, doesn't even bother to guard that knowledge which makes it the elite.' There is, he thought, probably a free pamphlet, distributed by UN-West for the asking, titled something like, HOW WE RULE YOU FELLAS AND WHAT ARE YOU GOING TO DO ABOUT IT?

'You're in authority,' Maren reminded him.

Glancing at her he said, 'You do keep that telepathic brain-add turned on. Despite Behren's Ordinance.'

Maren said, 'It cost me fifty mil to get it installed. You think I'm going to set it to the *off* position, really? Look how it earns its keep. It tells me if you're faithful or off in some conapt with —'

'Read my subconscious, then.'

'I have been. Anyhow, why? Who wants to know where you keep the nasty things you don't want to know —'

'Read it anyhow! Read the prognosticating aspects. What

45

I'm going to do, the potential action still in germinal form.'

Maren shook her head. 'Such big words and such little ideas.'

She giggled at his response. The ship, now, on auto-auto, had reached a height above the commute-layer, was on its way out of town. He had reflexively instructed it to vacate Paris ... God knew why.

'I'll analyze you, dear duck,' she said. 'It's really touching, what you're thinking over and over again deep down there in that substandard mind of yours – substandard if you don't count that knob on the frontal lobe that makes you a medium.'

He waited to hear only the truth.

Maren said, 'Over and over again that little inner voice is squeaking, *Why* must the pursaps believe what isn't so? *Why* can't they be told, and being told, accept?' Her tone was compassionate, now. For her, quite unusually so. 'You just can't grasp the incredible truth. They can't.'

SEVEN

After dinner they made for Maren's Paris apartment. He prowled about in the living-room, waiting while Maren changed, as Jean Harlow once remarked in an ancient but still potent flick, 'into something more comfortable.'

Then he happened onto a device resting on a low imitation tarslewood table. It was vaguely familiar and he picked it up, handled it with curiosity. Familiar – and yet utterly strange.

The bedroom door was partly open, 'What's this?' he called. He could see her dim, underwear-clad form as she traveled back and forth between the bed and closet. 'This thing that looks like a human head with no features. The size of a baseball.'

Maren called back cheerfully, 'That's from 202.'

'My sketch?' He stared at the object. Plowshared. This was the product for the retail market derived from the decision of one concomody on the Board. 'What's it do?' he asked, finding no switches.

'It amuses.'

'How?'

Maren appeared in the doorway briefly, wearing nothing. 'Say something to it.'

Glancing at her, Lars said, 'I'm more amused just looking at you. There's about three pounds you've put on.'

'Ask,' Maren said, 'the Orville a question. Ol' Orville is the rage. People cloister themselves for days with it, doing nothing but asking and getting answers. It replaces religion.'

'There is no religion,' he said, feeling serious. His experiences with the hyper-dimensional realm had disabused him of any dogmatic or devotional faith. If anyone living was qualified to claim knowledge of the 'next world' it was he, and as yet he had discovered no transcendent aspect to it.

Maren said, 'Then tell it a joke.'

'Can't I just put it back where I found it?'

'You really don't care how they plowshare your items.'

'No, that's their business.' However, he tried to think of a joke. 'What has six eyes,' he said, 'is headed for entropy, wears a derby hat —'

'Can't you ask it a serious joke?' Maren said. She returned to the bedroom, resumed dressing. 'Lars, you're polymorphic perverse.'

'Um,' he said.

'In the bad sense. The instinct for self-destruction.'

'Better that,' he answered, 'than the instinct to murder.' Maybe he could ask Ol' Orville that question. He said to the hard, small sphere in his hand, 'Am I making a mistake by feeling sorry for myself? By fighting city hall? By talking with a Soviet official during my coffee break?' He waited; nothing occurred. 'By believing,' he said, 'that it is time that those who claim to be making machines to kill and maim and lay waste

47

ought to have the ethical integrity to really make machines that kill and maim and lay waste instead of machines that constitute an elaborate pretext to finally bring forth a nonentity, a decadent novelty, such as yourself?' Again he waited, but Ol' Orville remained silent.

'It's broken,' he called to Maren.

'Give it a second. It's got fourteen thousand minned parts in it; they have to function in sequence.'

'You mean the *entire guidance system* from 202?'

He stared at Ol' Orville with horror. Yes, of course; this sphere was precisely the size and shape of the guidance system of 202. He began thinking of the possibilities. It could solve problems, fed to it orally, rather than on punched or iron oxide tape, to a magnitude of sixty constituents. No wonder it was taking its time to answer him. He had activated a prize assembly.

Probably in no sketch would he exceed this. And now here it was, Ol' Orville, a novelty to fill the vacant time and brains of men and women whose jobs had degenerated into repetitive psychomotor activity on a level that a trained pigeon could better perform. God! His worst expectations were fulfilled!

Lars P., he thought, remembering Kafka's stories and novels, woke up one morning to discover that somehow overnight he had been transformed into a gigantic – what? Cockroach?

'What am I?' he asked Ol' Orville. 'Forget my previous queries; just answer that! What have I become?' He squeezed the sphere angrily.

Now dressed in blue-cotton Chinese pajama bottoms, Maren stood at the door of her bedroom observing him as he fought it out with Ol' Orville. 'Lars P. woke up one morning to discover that somehow overnight he had been transformed into a —' She broke off, because in the corner of the living room the TV set had said *pingggggg*. It was turning itself on. A news bulletin was about to be read.

Forgetting Ol' Orville, Lars and she turned to face the TV set. He felt his pulse speed up. News bulletins were almost always bad news.

The TV screen showed a fixed still reading NEWS BUL-

48

LETIN. The announcer's voice sounded professionally calm: 'NASBA, the Wes-bloc space agency at Cheyenne, Wyoming, announced today that a new satellite, presumably launched by Peoples' China or Freedom For Mankind Cuba, is in orbit at an —'

Maren turned the set off. 'Some news bulletin.'

'The day I'm waiting for,' Lars said, 'is when a satellite already up launches its own satellite by itself.'

'They do that now. Don't you read the 'papes? Don't you read *Scientific American*? Don't you know *anything*?' Her scorn was semi-serious, semi-not. 'You're an idiot savant, like those cretins who memorize license plates or all the vidphone numbers in the Los Angeles area or the zip-codes for every population center in North America.' She returned to the bedroom for the top to her pajamas.

In Lars' hand, forgotten, Ol' Orville stirred and spoke.

It was uncanny; he blinked as its telepathic verbal response croaked at him, its answer to a question he had already forgotten asking. 'Mr. Lars.'

'Yes,' he said, hypnotized.

Ol' Orville creakily unwound its long-labored-for results. Toy though it was, Ol' Orville was not facile. Too many components had gone into its make-up for it to be merely glib. 'Mr. Lars, you have posed an ontological query. The Indo-European linguistic structure involved defeats a fair analysis; would you rephrase your question?'

After a moment of thought he said, 'No, I wouldn't.'

Ol' Orville was silent and then it responded, 'Mr. Lars, you are a forked radish.'

For the life of him he did not know whether to laugh. 'Shakespeare,' he said, speaking to Maren who, now reasonably fully dressed, had joined him, was listening, too. 'It's quoting.'

'Of course. It relies on its enormous data-bank. What did you expect, a brand-new sonnet? It can only retail what it's been fed. It can only select, not invent.' Genuinely puzzled, Maren said, 'I honestly think, Lars, that all kidding aside, you really do *not* have a technical mind and really do *not* have any intellectual —'

'Be quiet,' he said. Ol' Orville had more to offer.

Ol' Orville whined draggingly, like a slowed-down disc, 'You also asked, "What have I become?" You have become an outcast. A wanderer. Homeless. To paraphrase Wagner —'

'Richard Wagner?' Lars asked. 'The composer?'

'And dramatist and poet,' Ol' Orville reminded him. 'In *Siegfried*, to paraphrase in order to depict your situation. *'Ich hab' nicht Bruder, noch Schwester, Meine Mutter —'*

Finishing, Ol' Orville said, '*– ken' Ich nicht. Mein Vater —'*

Then its assembly received, integrated and accepted Maren's remark; it shifted its electronic gears. 'The name "Mr Lars' fooled me; I thought it was Norse. Excuse me, Mr. Lars. I mean to say that, like Parsifal, you are *Waffenlos*, without weapons ... in two senses, figurative and literal. You do not actually make weapons, as your firm officially pretends. And you are *Waffenlos* in another, more vital sense. You are *defenseless*. Like the young Siegfried, before he slays the dragon, drinks its blood and understands the song of the bird, or, like Parsifal, before he learns his name from the flower maidens, you are innocent. In, perhaps, the bad sense.'

'Not the pure fool,' Maren said practically, nodding. 'I paid sixty poscreds for you. Go ahead and blab.'

She went off to get a cigarillo from the package on the coffee table.

Ol' Orville was chewing over a decision – as if it could decide, rather than, as Maren pointed out, merely select from the data installed in its file-banks. Finally it said, 'I know what you want. You face a dilemma. You are *in* a dilemma, *now*. But you have never articulated it to yourself, never faced it.'

'What in hell is it?' he demanded, baffled.

Ol' Orville said, 'Mr. Lars, you have a terrible fear that one day you will enter your New York office, lie down and enter your trance-state, and revive with no sketches to show. In other words, lose your talent.'

Except for Maren's faintly asthmatic breathing as she smoked her Garcia y Vega cigarillo, the room was silent.

'Gee,' Lars said, mollified. He felt like a small, small boy,

50

as if all the years of adulthood had been ripped away. It was an eerie experience.

Because of course this toy, this novelty-gadget which was a perversion of the original Mr. Lars, Incorporated design, was correct. His fear was a near-castration fear. And it never went away.

Ol' Orville was ponderously winding up its statement. 'Your conscious quandary as to the spuriousness of your so-called "weapons" designs is an artificial, false issue. It obscures the psychological reality beneath. You know perfectly well, as any sane human would, that there is absolutely no argument for producing *genuine* weapons, either in Wes-bloc or Peep-East. Mankind was saved from destruction when the two monoliths secretly met at plenipotentiary level in Fairfax, Iceland, in 1992, to agree on the "plowsharing"-principle, then openly in 2002 to ratify the Protocols.'

'Enough,' Lars said looking at the object.

Ol' Orville shut up.

Going to the coffee table Lars set the object back down, shakily. 'And this amuses the pursaps?' he asked Maren.

Maren said, 'They don't ask deep-type questions. They ask it dumb, gag-type questions. Well, well.' She eyed him intently. 'So all this time all this talk on your part, this moaning and groaning about, "God, I'm a fraud, I'm perpetrating a hoax on the poor pursaps," all that hog-wash —' she had flushed with indignation – 'was just so much gabble.'

'Evidently so,' Lars agreed, still shaken. 'But I didn't know it. I don't see any psychoanalysts – I hate them. They're frauds, too. Siegmund Fraud.'

He waited hopefully. She did not laugh.

'Castration fear,' she said. 'Fear of loss of virility. Lars, you're afraid that because your trance-state sketches are not designs for authentic weapons – you see, darling duck dear? You fear it means that you're impotent.'

He did not meet her gaze.

'*Waffenlos*,' he said. 'That's a polite euphemism —'

'All euphemisms are polite; that's what it means.'

'– for impotency. I'm not a man.' He stared at Maren.

'In bed,' Maren said, 'you're twelve men. Fourteen. Twenty. Just wow.' She gazed at him hopefully, to see if that cheered him.

'Thanks' he said. 'But the sense of failure remains. Perhaps even Ol' Orville hasn't actually penetrated to the root of the matter. Somehow Peep-East is involved.'

Maren said, 'Ask Ol' Orville.'

Once more picking up the featureless head, Lars said, 'What is it about Peep-East that figures in all this, Ol' Orville?'

A pause, while the complex electronic system whirred, and then the gadget responded. 'A blurred, distance-shot, glossy. Too blurred to tell you what you wish to know.'

At once Lars knew. And tried to eradicate the thought from his mind, because his mistress and co-worker Maren Faine was standing right there by him, picking up his thoughts, in defiance of Western law. Had she gotten it, or had he cut it off in time, buried it back in his unconscious where it belonged?

'Well, well,' Maren said thoughtfully. 'Lilo Topchev.'

He said, fatalistically, 'Yep.'

'In other words,' Maren said, and the magnitude of her intelligence, the reason for giving her a top-level spot in his organization, manifested itself – unfortunately for him, he thought dismally. 'In other words, you see the solution to the virility-sterility psycho-sexual weapons-designs dilemma in the most asinine way possible. In a way if you were say nineteen years old —'

'I'll go see a psychiatrist,' he said, lamely.

'You want a good clear pic of that goddam miserable little female communist snake?' Maren's voice was sharp with hate, blame, accusation, fury – everything muddled, but distinct enough to carry across the room to him and hit hard; he felt the impact, fully.

'Yep,' he said stoically.

'I'll get one for you. Okay, I will. I mean it. I'll do even better than that; I'll explain to you in simple, short words, the kind you can comprehend, how *you* can get it, because personally I'd prefer on second thought not to involve myself in

52

something so —' she searched for the word, the good, solid, below-the-belt punch – 'so soggy.'

'How?'

'First, face this: KACH will never, never get it for you. If they turned over a blurred shot they did it on purpose. They could have gotten a better one.'

'You've lost me.'

'KACH,' Maren said, as if speaking to a child, and one whom she had damn little sympathy with, 'is what they like to call *disinterested*. Strip this of its self-serving nobility and you get at the truth: KACH serves two masters.'

'Oh yes,' he said, understanding. 'Us and Peep-East.'

'They have to please everyone and offend no one. They're the Phoenicians of the modern world, the Rothschilds, the Fuggars. From KACH you can contract for espionage services, but – you get a blurred distance-shot of Lilo Topchev.' She sighed; it was so easy, and yet it had to be spelled out to him. 'Doesn't that remind you of anything, Lars? Think.'

At last he said, 'The pic Aksel Kaminsky had. Of sketch 265. It was inadequate.'

'Oh, darling. You *see*, you actually *see*.'

'And,' he said, carefully keeping himself unrattled, 'your theory is that it's policy. They deliver enough to keep both blocs buying, but not enough to offend anyone.'

'Right. Now look.' She seated herself, puffing agitatedly on her cigarillo. 'I love you, Lars; I want to keep you as mine, to fuss over and annoy; I adore annoying you because you're so annoyable. But I'm not greedy. Your psychological weak-links as Ol' Orville said is your fright that you've lost your virility. That makes you like every other male over the age of thirty ... you're slowing down just a teeny bit and that scares you; you sense the waning of the life-force. You're good in bed but not *quite* as good as last week or last month or last year. Your blood, your heart, your – well, anyhow, your body knows it and so your mind knows it. I'll help you.'

'Then help. Instead of orating,' he said.

'You contact this Aksel Kaminsky.'

He glanced up at her. Her expression showed she meant it;

53

she was nodding soberly.

'And,' she said, 'you say, Ivan – call him Ivan. It annoys them. Then he can call you Joe or Yank, but you don't care. Ivan, you say. You want to know detail about item 265. That is correct, Ivan? Okay, comrade from East; I give you detail and you give me pic of lady weapons fashion designer Miss Topchev. Good pic, in color, maybe even 3-D. Maybe, yes even film sequence so I can run off – with nice sound-track of voice – in evening to fill vacant leisure-hours. And maybe if you have stag-type film sequence of hot, pelvis-twitching in which she —'

'You think he'll do it?'

'Yes.'

Lars thought, and I head the firm; I employ this woman. Obviously in another year, and me with psychological problems already ... but I have the talent, the Psionic ability. So I can stay on top. He felt the insubstantiality of his over-all prowess, however, in confrontation with this woman, his mistress. Now that she had proposed, so quaintly phrased, too, the deal with Kaminsky it all seemed so obvious and yet – insanely, he would never have conjured it up on his own. Incredible!

And it would work.

EIGHT

On Thursday he spent the morning at Lanferman Associates, examining the mockups, prototypes and just plain fakes that the engineers had put together, the artists and draftsmen and poly-something experts and electronics geniuses and clear-cut madmen, the crowd that Jack Lanferman paid, and in a way which always struck Lars as eccentric.

Jack Lanferman never scrutinized the work done for him in exchange. He seemed to believe that if properly rewarded every human being of talent did his best, with no goad, no thrusts or kicks or fires, no interoffice memos, nothing.

And oddly, it appeared true. Because Jack Lánferman did not have to spend his time in his office. He lived almost constantly in one of his sybaritic pleasure-palaces, coming down to Earth only when it was time to view some finished product before its public release.

In this case what had originated as sketch 278 had now passed through all its confirmation stages and had been 'test-fired.' It was, among and in company with admittedly bizarre compeers, unique. On his own part, Lars Powderdry had never known whether to laugh or weep openly when he contemplated item 278, now termed more ominously – to please the pursaps, who would look upon it by this title only – the Psychic Conservation Beam.

Seated in the small theater somewhere under central California, with Pete Freid on one side of him Jack Lanferman on the other, Lars watched the Ampex video tape of the Psychic Conservation Beam in 'action.' Since it was an anti-personnel weapon it could not be used on some obsolete, hulking old battleship of a spacecraft floated out from orbit to be blown to bits at a distance of eleven million miles. The target had to be human beings. Along with everyone else, Lars disliked this part.

The Psychic Conservation Beam was being demonstrated as it sucked dry the mentalities of a gang of worthless-looking thugs who had been detected trying to seize control of a small, isolated (in other words, pathetically helpless) colony of Wes-bloc's on Ganymede.

On the screen the bad fellas froze, anticipating the tearwep – the instrument of terror. Rewarding, Lars thought. As a drama it was satisfying; because the bad fellas, up to this moment, had run riot through the colony. Like grotesques painted into existence as old-time movie ads, to be pasted up at the entrances of local neighborhood theaters, the bad fellas had torn the clothing from young girls, beaten old men into indistinct blobs, had set fire drunken-soldierwise to venerable buildings ... had done, Lars decided, everything except burn the library at Alexandria with its sixteen thousand priceless irreplaceable scrolls, including four lost-forever tragedies of Sophocles.

'Jack,' he said to Lanferman, 'couldn't you have set it in ancient Hellenistic Palestine? You know how sentimental the pursaps are about that period.'

'I know,' Lanferman agreed. 'That's when Socrates was put to death.'

'Not quite,' Lars said. 'But that's the general idea. Couldn't you have your androids shown as they laser down Socrates? What a powerful scene that would make. Of course you'd have to supply subtitles or dub in an English voice-track. So the pursaps could hear Socrates' pleas.'

Pete murmured, absorbed in watching the video tape, 'He didn't plead; he was a stoic.'

'Okay,' Lars said. 'But at least he could look worried.'

Now the FBI, using item 278, for the first time in history, as the film took pains to inform its audience via the calm commentary by none other than Lucky Bagman himself, swooped. The bad fellas blanched, groped for their antiquated laser pistols or whatever it was they had – perhaps Frontier Model Colt .44s, Lars thought acidly. Anyhow it was all over for them.

And the results would have moved, or in this case melted, a stone.

It was worse that the Fall of the House of Atreus, Lars decided. Blindness, incest, daughters and sisters torn apart by wild beasts ... what reality, in the final analysis, was the worst fate that could befall a group of humans? Slow starvation, as in the Nazi concentration camps, accompanied by beatings, impossibly hard work, arbitrary indignities and at last the 'shower baths' which were actually Zyklon B hydrogen cyanide gas chambers?

Yet item 278 nonetheless added to mankind's fund of techniques. Tools to injure and degrade. Aristotle on all fours, ridden like a donkey, with a bit between his teeth. Such the pursaps wanted; such was evidently their pleasure. Or was this all a hideous, fundamentally wrong guess?

Wes-bloc, its ruling elite, believed that the people were comforted by this sort of video tape, shown – incredibly – at the dinner hour, displayed in still form or via color pic in the breakfast-time 'pape, to be ingested along with the eggs and toast. *The pursaps liked displays of power because they felt powerless themselves.* It heartened them to see Item 278 make mincemeat out of a gang of thugs who were beyond the pale. Item 278, from FBI high-muzzle-velocity guns, sped out in the form of thermotropic darts which found their targets —

And Lars looked away.

'Androids,' Pete reminded him laconically.

Lars said between his teeth, 'They look human to me.'

The film, horrid to Lars, clanked on. Now the bad fellas, like husks, like dehydrated skins, deflated bladders, wandered about; they neither saw nor heard. Instead of a satellite or a building or a city being blown up a group of human brains, candle-like, had been blown out.

'I want out,' Lars said.

Jack Lanferman looked sympathetic. 'Frankly I don't know why you came in here at all. Go out and get a Coke.'

'He has to watch,' Pete Freid said. 'He's taking responsibility.'

'All right.' Jack nodded reasonably, hunching forward and tapping Lars on the knee to gain his shattered attention. 'Look, my friend. *It isn't as if 278 will ever be used.* It isn't as if —'

'It is as if,' Lars said. 'It's goddam completely, as if you could make it. I have an idea. Run the tape backward.'

Jack and Pete glanced at each other, then at him expectantly. After all, you never knew; even a sick man might have a good idea now and then. A man made temporarily ill.

'First you show these people like they are now,' Lars said. 'As mindless, de-brained, reduced to reflex-machines, with maybe the upper ganglia of the spinal column intact, nothing more. That's how they start out. Then the FBI ships spurt the essential quality of humanness back into them. Got it? Have I found a winner?'

Jack giggled. 'Funny. You'd have to call it a Psychic Bestower Gun. But it wouldn't work.'

'Why not?' Lars said. 'If I were a pursap I know it would comfort me to see human qualities imparted to de-brained wrecks. Wouldn't it comfort you?'

'But see, my friend,' Jack pointed out patiently, 'what would emerge as a result of the item's action would be a gang of hoodlums.

True. He had forgotten about that.

However, Pete spoke up at this point, and on his side. 'But they wouldn't be hoodlums if the tape was run backward because they'd set museums un-on fire, undetonate hospitals, reclothe the nubile bodies of naked young girls, restore the punched-in faces of old men. And just generally bring the dead to life, in a sort of off-hand manner.'

Jack said, 'It would spoil the pursaps' dinners to watch it.' He spoke with finality. With authority.

'What makes pursaps tick?' Lars asked him. Jack Lanferman would know; it was Jack's job to know that. He lived by means of that knowledge.

Without hesitation Jack said, 'Love.'

'Then why this?' Lars gestured at the screen. Now the FBI was carting off the hulks who had been men, rounding them up like so many stunned steers.

'The pursap,' Jack said thoughtfully, in a tone that told Lars that this was no light answer, no frivolity, 'is afraid in the back of his mind that weapons like this exist. If we didn't show them, the pursap would believe in their existence anyhow. And he'd be afraid that somehow, for reasons obscure to him, they might be used on him. Maybe he didn't pay his jethopper license fee on time. Or maybe he cheated on his income tax. Or maybe – maybe he knows, deep down inside him, that he's not the way God built him originally. That in some way he doesn't quite fathom, he's corrupt.'

'Deserves item 278 turned his way.' Pete said, nodding.

'But he's wrong,' Lars said futilely. 'He doesn't deserve

anything, anything at all, remotely like 278 or 240 or 210, any of them. He doesn't and they don't.' He gestured at the screen.

'But 278 exists,' Jack said. 'The pursap knows it, and when he sees it used on an uglier life form than him he thinks, Hey. Maybe they passed me by. Maybe because those fellas are so really bad, those Peep-East bastards, 278 isn't going to get pointed at me and I can go to my grave later on, not this year but say fifty years from now. Which means – and this is the crux, Lars – he doesn't have to worry about his own death right now. *He can pretend he will never die.*'

After a pause Pete said somberly. 'The only event that really makes him secure, makes him *really* believe he's going to survive, is to see another person get it *in his place*. Someone else, Lars, had died for him.'

Lars said nothing. What was there to say? It sounded right; both Pete and Jack agreed, and they were professionals: they went about their jobs intentionally, rationally, whereas he, as Maren had pointed out, was an idiot savant. He had a talent, but nothing – absolutely nothing, did he know. If Pete and Jack said this, then all he could do was nod.

'The only mistake ever made in this area,' Jack said presently, 'in the field of tearweps, was the mid-twentieth century inanity, insanity, of the universal weapon. The bomb that blew *everyone* up. That was a *real* mistake. That went too far. That had to be reversed. So we got tactical weapons. Specialized more and more – especially in the tearwep class, so that not only could they pick out their target but they could get at you emotionally. I go for tearweps; I understand the idea. But localization: that's the essence.' He put on, for effect, his clumsy ethnic accent. 'You don't got no target, Meester Lars, sir, when you got zap gun which blow up whole world, even though it make lot of plenty fine terror. You got —' He grinned wise-peasantishly. 'You got hammer with which you hit yourself over your own head.'

The accent and the attempt at humor were gone, as he said, 'The H-bomb was a monstrous, paranoid-logic error. The product of a paranoid nut.'

'There are not nuts like that alive today,' Pete said quietly.

Jack said instantly, 'That we know of.'

The three of them glanced at one another.

Across the continent Surley G. Febbs said, 'A one-way express first-class window-seat ticket on a 66-G no-blowby rocket to Festung, Washington, D.C. And snap it up, miss.' He carefully laid out a ninety poscred note on the brass surface before the TWA clerk's window.

NINE

Behind Surley G. Febbs in the line at the TWA ticket-reservations-baggage window a portly, well-cloaked, businessman-type was saying to the individual behind *him*, 'Look at this. Get a load of what's going on overhead behind our backs right this minute. A new satellite in orbit, and by them. Not us.' He refolded page one of his morning homeopape, to show.

'Chrissake,' the man behind him said dutifully. Naturally Surley G. Febbs, while he waited for his ticket to Festung, Washington, D.C. to be validated, listened in. Naturally.

'Wonder if it's a hedgehog,' the portly businessman-type said.

'Naw.' The individual behind him shook his head vigorously. 'We'd object. You suppose a man of General George Nitz' stature would allow that? We'd register an official government protest so fast —'

Turning, Surley Febbs said, ' "Protest"? Are you kidding? Is that the kind of leaders we have? You actually believe what's needed is *words*? If Peep-East put that satellite up without officially registering the specs with SINK-PA in advance we'll —' he gestured – 'Whammo. Down it comes.'

He received his ticket and change from the clerk.

Later, in the express jet, first-class accommodation, window seat, he found himself next to the portly, well-cloaked, businessman-type. After a few seconds – the flight in all lasted only fifteen minutes – they resumed their conversation of solemn weight. They were now passing over Colorado and the Rockies could be seen below, briefly, but due to the nobility of their discussion they ignored that great range. It would be there later on, but *they* might not be. This was urgent.

Febbs said, 'Hedgehog or not, every Peep miss is a men.'

'Eh?' the portly businessman said.

'Every Peep-East missile is a menace. They're all up to something.' Something evil, he said to himself, and glanced at the portly man's 'pape, over his shoulder. 'I see it's a type never before seen. God knows what it might contain. Frankly, I think we ought to drop a Garbage-can Banger on New Moscow.'

'What's *that*?'

Condescendingly, because he fully realized that the average man had not done research endlessly at the pub-libe as he had, Febbs said, 'It's a missile that wide-cracks in the atmosphere. "Atmosphere," from the Sanskrit *atmen*, "breath." The word "Sanskrit" from *samskrta*, meaning "cultivated," which is from *sama*, meaning "equal," plus *kr*, "to do," and *krp*, "form." In the atmosphere, anyhow, above the popcen – the population center – which it's aimed at. We place the Judas Iscariot IV above New Moscow, set to wide-crack at half a mile, and it rains down minned – miniaturized – h'd, that means homeostatic —'

It was hard to communicate with the ordinary mass man. Nonetheless Febbs did his best to find terms which this portly nonentity – this nont – would comprehend. 'They're about the size of gum wrappers. They drift throughout the city, especially into the rings of conapts. You do know what a conapt is, don't you?'

Spluttering, the portly businessman-type said, 'I live in one.'

Febbs, unperturbed, continued his useful exposition. 'They're cam – that is, chameleon; they blend, colorwise, with whatever they land on. So you can't detect them. There they lie, until nightfall, say around ten o'clock at night.'

'How do they know when it's ten o'o'clock? Each has a wristwatch?' The portly businessman's tone was faintly sneering, as if he imagined that somehow Febbs was putting him on.

With massive condescension Febbs said, 'By the loss of heat in the atmosphere.'

'Oh.'

'About ten p.m., when everyone's asleep.' Febbs gloated in the thought of this strategic weapon in action, its precision. It was a thin road which this weapon laid, like the gate to salvation; esthetically it was satisfying. You could enjoy knowing about this Garbage-can Banger even without its actually going into operation.

'Okay,' the portly man said. 'So at ten p.m. —'

'They start,' Febbs said. 'Each pellet, fully cammed, begins to emit a sound.' He watched the portly man's face. Obviously this citizen did not bother to read *Wep Weke*, the info mag devoted exclusively to pics and articles, and, where possible, true specs, of all new weapons, both Wes-bloc and Peep-East – probably by means of a data-collecting agency he had in a vague way heard of named KICH or KUCH or KECH. Febbs had a ten-year file of *Wep Weke*, complete, with both front and back covers intact; it was priceless.

'What kind of sound?'

'A horrid sneering sound. Buzzing. Like – well, you'd have to hear it yourself. The point is, it keeps you awake. And I don't mean just a little awake. I mean *wide*-awake. Once the noise of a Garbage-can Banger gets to you, for example, if a pellet is on the roof of your conapt building, you never sleep again. And four days without sleeping —' He snapped his fingers. 'You can't perform your job. You're no good to anyone, yourself included.'

'Fantastic.'

'And,' Febbs said, 'the chances are good that pellets might land and immediately cam in the vicinity of the villa of a SeRKeb member. And that could mean the collapse of the

62

government.'

'But,' the portly man said, with a trace of worry, 'don't *they* have hardware equally sinister? I mean —'

'Peep-East,' Febbs said, 'would retaliate. Naturally. Probably they'd try out their Sheep Dip Isolator.'

'Oh yeah,' the portly businessman said, nodding. 'I've read about that. They used it when their colony on Io revolted last year.'

'We in the West,' Febbs said, 'have never smelled the Sheep Dip Isolator's implementing irritant. It's said to defy description.'

'I read somewhere that a rat that's died in the wall —'

'Far worse. I admit they have something there. It descends in the form of condensation from a Type VI Julian the Apostate satellite. The drops spatter in an area of say ten square miles. And wherever they land they penetrate inter-mol-wise – intermolecularly – and can't be eradicated, even by Supsolv-x, that new detergent we have. Nothing works.'

He spoke calmly, showing that he faced this tearwep without blenching. It was a fact of life, like going regularly to the dentist; Peep-East possessed it, might use it, but even this Sheep Dip Isolator could be matched by something of Wesbloc's that was more effective.

But he could imagine the Sheep Dip Isolator in Boise, Idaho. The effect on the million citizens of the city. They would awaken to the stench, and it would be inter-mol everywhere, on and in buildings, in sub-supra- and surface-vehicles, autofacs – and the stench would drive one million people out of the city. Boise, Idaho would become a ghost city, inhabited only by autonomic mechanisms still grinding away uncursed by the possession of noses – and by *the smell*.

It made you stop and think.

'But they won't use it,' Febbs decided, aloud. 'Because we could retaliate with, for instance —'

He scanned the fantastically extensive data-collection imbedded in his mind. He could envision a host of retalweps which would make the Sheep Dip Isolator small spuds indeed. 'We'd try,' he pronounced decisively, as if it were up to him, 'the Civic Notification Distorter.'

'Chrissake, what's *that*?'

'The final solution,' Febbs said, 'in my opinion, in n-e weapons.' N-e: that signified the esoteric term, used in Wes-bloc's weapons-circles such as the Board which he now (God in his wisdom be praised!) belonged to, needle-eye. And needle-eyeification was the fundamental direction which weapons had been taking for a near-half-century. It meant, simply, weapons with the most precise effect conceivable. In theory it was possible to imagine a weapon – as yet unbuilt, probably untranced of by Mr. Lars himself, still – that would slay one given individual at a given instant at a given inter-section in one particular given city in Peep-East. Or in Wes-bloc, for that matter. Peep-East, Wes-bloc: what difference did it make? The important thing would be the existence of the weapon itself. The *perfect* weapon.

God, how clearly he could conceive it in his own mind. One would sit down – *he* would – in a room. Before him, a control panel with dials ... and one single button. He would read the dials, note the settings. Time, space, the synchronicity of the dimensional factors would move toward fusion. And Gafne Rostow (that was the everyman name for the average enemy citizen) would walk briskly toward that spot, to arrive at that time. He Febbs, would press the button and Gafne Rostow would —

Hmm. Would disappear? No, that was to maj. Too magical. Not in accord with the reality-situation. Gafne Rostow, a minor bureaucrat in some temporary, small-budget ministry of the Soviet Government, someone with a rubber stamp, desk, cramped office – he wouldn't just disappear; he would be *converted*.

This was the part which made Febbs shiver with relish. He did so now, causing the portly gentleman beside him to with-draw slightly and raise an eyebrow.

'Converted,' Febbs said, 'into a rug.'

The portly businessman stared.

'A rug,' Febbs repeated, irritably. 'Don't you understand? Or has the Judaeo-Christian tradition impaired your judgment? What kind of patriot are you?'

'I'm a patriot,' the portly businessman said, defensively.

'With glass eyes,' Febbs said. 'Natural-simulated. Of course if it didn't have good teeth, regular and white, if there were unsightly fillings or you couldn't get the yellow stain removed, it could be a wall-hanging. Flat.' The head could be discarded.

The portly businessman began, uneasily, to read his 'pape.

'I'll give you the poop,' Febbs said, 'on the Civic Notification Distorter. It's n-e but not terror. Not terminal. I mean it doesn't kill. It's in the conf class.'

'I know what that means,' the portly gentleman said hurriedly, keeping his eyes on the homeopape. Obviously he did not care to continue the discussion – for reasons which eluded Febbs. Perhaps, Febbs decided, the man felt guilty at his ignorance on this vital topic. 'That means confusions. Disorienting.'

'The Civic Notification Distorter,' Febbs said, 'bases its operation on the requirement that in present-day society every filled-out official form has to be recorded, microwise, in trio or quad or quin. Three, four or five copies *in every instance* have to be made. The weapon functions in a relatively uncomplicated manner. All micro-copies, after being Xeroxed, are carried over coaxial lines to file-repositories, generally subsurface and away from population centers, in case of a major war. You know, so they'll survive I mean, records have *got* to survive. So the Civic Notification Distorter is launched ground-to-ground say from Newfoundland to Peking. I've selected Peking because that's the Sino-South-Asia civic-institution concentration for that half of Peep-East; that's where *their* half of their total records originate. It strikes, screwing itself within a matter of microseconds out of sight in the ground; no visible trace survives. And at once it extends pseudopodia which search out, subsurface, until it contacts a co-ax carrying data to an archive. You see?'

'Um,' the portly businessman said, half-heartedly, trying to read. 'Say, this new satellite's design suggests possibly it even —'

'And the distorter,' Febbs said, 'Operates from that instant on in a way for which the word "inspired" is not excessive. It diverts integers of the data, the fundamental message-units, so that they no longer agree. In other words, copy two of the original document no longer can be superimposed on copy one. Copy three disagrees with copy two at one higher order of distortion. If a fourth copy exists it is reconstituted so that —'

'If you know so much about weapons,' the portly business-man broke in disagreeably, 'why aren't you in Festung, Washington, D.C.?'

Surley G. Febbs, with the mere trace of a smile, said, 'I am, fella. Wait and see. You're going to hear about me. Remember the name Surley G. Febbs. Got it? Surley Febbs. F as in fungus.'

The portly businessman said, 'Just tell me one thing. Then frankly, Mr. Febbs, F as in fungus, I don't want to hear any more; I can't take any more in. You said "rug." What was that? Why a rug? "Glass eyes," you said. And something about "natural simulated."' Uneasily, with tangible aversion, he said, 'You mean?'

'I mean,' Febbs said quietly, 'that something should remain as a reminder. So you know you achieved it.' He searched for, found the proper term to express his emotions, his intent. 'A trophy.'

The loudspeaker blurted, 'We are now landing at Abraham Lincoln Field. Surface travel to Festung, Washington, D.C. thirty-five miles to the east is available at slight additional cost; retain your ticket-receipt in order to qualify for low, low fares.'

Febbs glanced out the window for the first time during the trip and saw below him, gratifyingly, his new abode, the enormous, sprawling population center which was the capital of Wes-bloc. The source from which all authority emanated. Authority which he now shared.

And with the fund of his knowledge the world situation would rapidly pick up. He could, on the basis of this con-versation, foresee that.

Wait until I sit in on the top-security closed-session Board meetings down in the subsurface *kremlin* with General Nitz

66

and Mr. Lars and the rest of those fellas, he said to himself. The balance of power between East and West is going to radically alter. And boy, are they going to know about it in New Moscow and Peking and Havana.

The ship, retrojets whistling, began to descend.

But how best, Febbs inquired of himself, can I really serve my power-bloc? I'm not going to receive that one-sixth slice, that one component, which a concomody is asked to plowshare. That's not enough for *me*. Not after this conversation. It's made me see things straight. I'm a top weapons expert – although, admittedly, I don't have one of those formal degrees from some university or the Air Arm Military Academy at Cheyenne. Plowsharing? Is *that* all I can offer in the way of unique knowledge and talent so exceptional that you'd have to go back to the Roman Empire and even before to find its equal?

Hell no, he realized. Plowsharing is for the *average* man. I'm that, computerwise, statistically-speaking, but underneath that I'm Surley Grant Febbs, as I just now said to this man beside me. There are a lot of average men. Six always sit on the Board. But there's only Surley Febbs.

I want the complete weapon.

And when I get there and sit with them officially I'm going to get my hands on it. Whether they like it or not.

TEN

As Lars Powderdry and the others emerged from the theater in which the video tape of item 278 had been run, a loitering figure approached them.

'Mr. Lanferman?' Gasping for breath, eyes like sewn-on

buttons, the football-shaped, ill-dressed, broken reed sort of individual was lugging an enormous sample-case. He wedged himself in their path, blocking all escape. 'I just want a minute. Just let me say a couple of things – okay?'

It was one of Jack Lanferman's headaches, an encounter with marginal operators such as this man, Vincent Klug. Under the circumstances it was hard to know whom to feel more sorry for, Jack Lanferman who was big, powerful and expensive, as well as busy, with no idle time to spare, in that as a hedonist his time was convertible into physical pleasure and that was that. Or for Klug.

For years Vincent Klug had hung around. God knew how he gained access to the subsurface portion of Lanferman Associates. Probably someone at a minor post had been moved to pity and opened the floodgate a bare inch, recognizing that if not let in, Klug would remain a careless pest, would never give up. But this act of rather self-serving compassion by one of Lanferman's tiny above-surface employees merely transferred the pest-problem one level down – literally. Or up, if you viewed it figuratively. Because now Klug was so positioned as to bother the boss.

It was Klug's contention that the world needs toys.

This was his answer to whatever riddle the serious members of society confronted themselves with: poverty, deranged sex-crimes, senility, altered genes from over-exposure to radiation ... you name the problem and Klug opened his enormous sample-case and hauled out the solution. Lars had heard the toymaker expound this on several occasions: life itself was unendurable and hence had to be ameliorated. As a thing-in-itself it could not actually be lived. There had to be some way out. Mental, moral and physical hygiene demanded it.

'Look at this,' Klug said wheezingly to Jack Lanferman, who had halted indulgently, for the moment at least. Klug knelt down, deposited a miniature figure on the corridor floor. With blurred speed he added one after another more until a dozen figures stood ganged together, and then Klug presented the small assembly with a citadel.

There was no doubt; the citadel was an armed fortress. Not

archaic – not, for instance, a medieval castle – and yet not contemporary either. It was fanciful, and Lars was intrigued.

'This particular game,' Klug explained, 'is called Capture. These here —' he indicated the dozen figures, which Lars now discovered were oddly uniformed soldiers – 'they want to get in. And it —' Klug indicated the citadel – 'it wants to keep them out. If any one of them, just *one*, manages to get inside, the game's over. The attackers have won. But if the Monitor —'

'The what?' Jack Lanferman said.

'This.' Klug patted the citadel affectionately. 'I spent six months wiring it. If this destroys all twelve attacking troops, then the defenders have won. Now.'

From his sample-case he produced another item. 'This is the nexus through which the player operates either the attackers, if that's the side he's chosen, or the Monitor, if he's going to be the defenders.'

He held the objects toward Jack, who, however, declined. 'Well,' Klug said philosophically, 'anyhow this is a sample computer that even a seven-year-old can program. Any number up to six can play. The players take turns —'

'All right,' Jack Lanferman said patiently. 'You've built a prototype. Now what do you want me to do?'

Rapidly Klug said, 'I want it analyzed to see how much it would cost to autofac. In lots of five hundred. As a starter. And I'd like to see it run on your 'facs, because yours are the best in the world.'

'I know that,' Lanferman said.

'Will you do it?'

Lanferman said, 'You couldn't afford to pay me to cost-analyze this item. And if you could, you couldn't even begin to put up the retainer necessary if I were to have my 'facs run off even fifty, let alone five hundred. You know that, Klug.'

Swallowing, perspiring, Klug hesitated and then said, 'My credit's no good, Jack?'

'Your credit's good. *Any* credit is good. But you don't have any. You don't even know what the word means. Credit means —'

'I know,' Klug broke in. 'It means the ability to play later for what's bought now. But if I had five hundred of the number ready for the Fall market —'

'Let me ask you something,' Lanferman said.

'Sure, Jack. Mr. Lanferman.'

'How in that strange brain of yours, do you conceive a method by which you can advertise? This would be a high-cost item at every level, especially at retail. You couldn't merchandise it through one buyer for a chain of autodepts. It would have to go to cog-class families and be exposed in cog mags. And that's expensive.'

'Hmm,' Klug said.

Lars spoke up. 'Klug, let me ask you something.'

'Mr. Lars.' Klug extended his hand eagerly.

'Do you honestly believe that a war-game constitutes a morally adequate product to deliver over to children? Can you fit this into that theory of yours about "ameliorating the iniquities of modern —"'

'Oh wait,' Klug said, raising his hand. 'Wait, Mr. Lars.'

'I'm waiting.' He waited.

'Through capture the child learns the futility of war.'

Lars eyed him skeptically. Like hell he does, he thought.

'I mean it.' Vigorously, Klug's head bobbed up and down in a convinced determined nod of self-assent. 'Listen, Mr. Lars; *I know the story.* Temporarily, I admit it, my firm is in bankruptcy, but I still have cog inside knowledge. I understand, and I'm sympathetic. Believe me. I'm really very, totally sympathetic; I couldn't agree more with what you're doing. Honestly.'

'What am I doing?'

'I don't merely mean you, Mr. Lars, although you're one of the foremost —' Klug groped urgently for the means to express his fervid ideas, now that he had ensnared an audience. To Klug, Lars observed, an audience consisted of anyone above the number of zero, and above the age of two. Cog and pursap alike; Klug would have pleaded with them all. Because what he was doing, what he wanted, was so important.

Pete Freid said, 'Make a model for some *simple* toy, Klug.'

His tone was gentle. 'Something the auto-dept networks can market for a couple of beans. With maybe one moving part. You'd run off a few thousand for him, wouldn't you, Jack? If he brought in a really simple piece?'

To Vincent Klug he said, 'Give me specs and I'll build the prototype for you and maybe get a cost analysis.' To Jack he quickly explained, 'I mean on my own time, of course.'

Sighing, Lanferman said, 'You can use our shops. But please for God's sake don't kill yourself trying to bail out this guy. Klug was in the toy business, and a goddam failure, before you were out of college. He's had a hatful of chances and muffed every one.'

Klug stared at the floor drearily.

'I'm one of the foremost what?' Lars asked him.

Without rasing his head Klug said, 'The foremost healing and constructive forces in our sick society. And you, who are so few, must never be harmed.'

After a suitable interval Lars, Pete Freid and Jack Lanferman howled with laughter.

'Okay,' Klug said. With a sort of miserable, beaten-dog, philosophic slumped shrug he began gathering up his twelve tiny soldiers and his Monitor-citadel. He looked ever increasingly glum and deflated, and clearly he was going to leave – which, for him, was unusual. In fact unheard of.

Lars said, 'Don't interpret our reaction as —'

'It's not misunderstood,' Klug said in a faraway voice. 'The last thing any of you wants to hear is that you're *not* pandering to the sick inclinations of a depraved society. It's easier for you to pretend you've been bought by a bad system.'

'I never heard such strange logic in my life,' Jack Lanferman said, genuinely puzzled. 'Have you, Lars?'

Lars said, 'I think I know what he means, only he's not able to say it. Klug means that we're in weapons design and manufacture and so we feel we've got to be tough. It's our great and bounden duty, as the Common Prayer Book says. People who invent and implement devices and blow up other people should be cynical. Only the fact is we're loveable.'

'Yes,' Klug said, nodding. 'That's the word. Love is the

71

basis of your lives, all three of you. You all share it, but especially you, Lars. Compare yourselves to the dreadful police and military agencies who are the real and awful personages in power. Compare your motivation to KACH in particular, and the FBI and KVB. SeRKeb and Natsec. Their basis —'

'Upper gastro-intestinal irritation is the basis of my life,' Pete said. 'Especially late Saturday night.'

Jack said, 'I have colonic trouble.'

'I have a chronic urinary infection,' Lars said. 'Bacteria keep forming, in particular if I drink too much orange juice.'

Sadly, Klug snapped his huge sample-case shut. 'Well, Mr. Lanferman,' he said as he walked gradually off sagging with the weight of the loaded case as if the air were slowly leaking out of him, 'I appreciate your time.'

Pete said, 'Remember what I said, Klug. Give me something with *just one moving part* and I'll —'

'Thank you very much,' Klug said and, with a sort of vague dignity, turned the corner of the corridor. He was gone.

'Out of his mind,' Jack said after a pause. 'Look what Pete offered him: his time and skill. And I offered him the use of our shops. And he walked off.' Jack shook his head. 'I don't get it. I don't really understand what makes that guy tick. After all these years.'

'Are we really loveable?' Pete asked. 'I mean seriously; I want to know. Somebody say.'

The final, irrefutable answer came from Jack Lanferman. 'What the hell does it matter?' Jack said.

ELEVEN

And yet it did matter, Lars thought as he rode by high-velocity express back from San Francisco to his office in New York. Two principles governed history: the power-inspired and the – what Klug said – the healing principle, idly referred to as 'love.'

Reflexively he examined the late edition 'pape placed considerately before him by the hostess. It had one good big headline:

New Sat Not Peep-East, says SeRKeb Speculation Planet-Wide as to Origin UN-W NATSEC Asked to Investigate.

They who had asked, Lars discovered, were a mysterious, dim organization called the 'United States Senate.' Spokesman: a transparent shade named President Nathan Schwarzkopf. Like the League of Nations, such bodies perpetuated themselves, even though they had ceased to be even a chowder and marching society.

And in the USSR, an equally insubstantial entity called the Supreme Soviet had by now yelped nervously for someone to take an interest in the unaccounted-for new satellite, one among over seven hundred, but still a peculiar one.

'May I have a phone?' Lars asked the ship's hostess.

A vidphone was brought to his seat, plugged in. Presently he was talking to the screening sharpy at the switchboard at Festung, Washington, D.C.

'Let me have General Nitz.' He gave his cog-code, all twenty portions of it, verifying it by inserting his thumb into the slot of the vidphone. The miles of strung-together gimmicks analyzed and transmitted his print and, at the switchboard in the subsurface *Kremlin*, the autonomic circuit switched him obediently to the human functionary who stood first in the long progression which acted as a shield between General Nitz and – well, reality.

The express ship had begun its gliding, slow descent at Wayne Morse Field in New York by the time Lars got through to General Nitz.

The carrot-shaped face materialized, wide at the top, tapering to a near-point, with horizontal, slubby, deeply countersunk eyes and gray hair that looked – and might well be – gummed in place, being artificial. And then, hooking in a stricture at the trachea, that wonderful insignia-impregnated hard-as-black-iron hoop collar. The medals themselves, awesome to behold, were not immediately visible. They lay below the scanner of the vid-camera.

'General,' Lars said, 'I assume the Board is in session. Shall I come directly there?'

Sardonically – it was his natural mode of address – General Nitz purred, 'Why, Mr. Lars? Tell me why. Had you intended to reach them by floating to the ceiling of the seccon chamber or having the conference table-rap spirit messages?'

'"Them,"' Lars said, disconcerted. 'Who do you mean, General?'

General Nitz rang off without answering.

The empty screen faced Lars like a vacuity echoing the tone of Nitz' voice.

Of course, Lars reflected, in a situation of this magnitude he himself did not count. General Nitz had too much else to worry about.

Shaken, Lars sat back and endured the rather rough landing of the ship, a hurried landing as if the pilot was eager to get his vessel out of the sky. Now would not be the time to 'coat to Peep-East, he thought drily. They're probably as nerve-wracked as UN-W Natsec, if not more so ... if it's true that they didn't put that satellite up. And evidently we believe them.

And they, in return, believe *us*. Thank God we can communicate back and forth to that degree. Undoubtedly both blocs have checked out the small fry: France and Israel and

Egypt and the Turks. It's not any of them either. So it's no one. Q.E.D.

On foot he crossed the drafty landing field and hailed an autonomic hopper car.

'Your destination, sir or madam?' the hopper car inquired as he crawled into it.

It was a good question. He did not feel like going to Mr. Lars, Incorporated. Whatever it was that was going on in the sky dwarfed his commercial activities – dwarfed even the activities of the Board, evidently. He could probably induce the hopper car to take him all the way to Festung, Washington, D.C. – which probably, despite General Nitz' sarcasm, was where he belonged. He was, after all, a bona fide member of the Board and when it sat in formal session he should by rights be present. But —

I'm not needed, he realized. It was as simple as that.

'Do you know a good bar?' he asked the hopper car.

'Yes, sir or madam,' the autonomic circuit of the hopper car answered. 'But it is only eleven in the morning. Only a drunk drinks at eleven in the morning.'

'But I'm scared,' Lars said.

'Why, sir or madam?'

Lars said, 'Because *they're* scared.' My client, he thought. Or employer or whatever the Board is. There anxiety has gotten down, all the way along the line, until it's reached to me. In that case I wonder how the pursaps feel, he wondered.

Is ignorance any help in this situation.

'Give me a vidphone,' he instructed the car.

A vidphone slid creakily out, to repose leadenly in his lap, and he dialed Maren, at the Paris branch.

'You heard?' he said, when her face at last appeared before him in gray miniature. It was not even a color vidphone – the circuit was that archaic.

Maren said, 'I'm glad you called! All kinds of stuff is showing up at the, you know, Greyhound bus station locker at Topeka, out of Geldthaler Gemeinschaft. From *them*. It's incredible.'

'This is not a mistake?' Lars broke in. 'They did not put up that new sat?'

'They swear. They affirm. They beg us to believe. No. In the name of God. Mother. The soil of Russia. You name it. The insane thing is that they, and I'm talking about the most responsible officials, the entire twenty-five men and women on SeRKeb, they're actually groveling. No dignity, no reserve. Maybe they have unbelievably guilty consciences; I don't know.' She looked weary; her eyes had lost their glitter.

'No,' he said. 'It's the Slavic temperament. It's a manner of address, like their invective. What specifically do they propose? Or has that gone directly to the Board and not through us?'

'Straight to Festung. All the lines are open, lines that are so gucked up with rust that it's impossible they'd carry a signal, and yet they are. They're now in use – maybe because everybody at the other end is yelling so loud. Lars, honest to God, one of them actually *cried*.'

Lars said, 'Under the circumstances it's easy to understand why Nitz hung up on me.'

'You talked to him? You actually got through? Listen.' Her voice was controlled by her intensity. 'An attempt has already been made to deposit weapons on the alien satellite.'

'Alien,' he echoed, dazed.

'And the robot weapons teams vanished. They were protected right up to their scalps, but they're just not there any more.'

'Probably returned to hydrogen atoms,' Lars said.

'It was our coup,' Maren said. 'Lars?'

'Yes.'

'That Soviet official who blubbered. It was a Red Army man.'

'The thing that gets me,' Lars said, 'is that all at once I'm on the outside, like Vincent Klug. It's a really terrible feeling.'

'You want to do something. And you can't even blubber.'

He nodded.

'Lars,' Maren said, 'do you understand? Everyone's on the outside; the Board, the SerRKeb – *they're* on the outside:

there *is* no inside. Not here, anyhow. That's why I'm already hearing the word "alien." It's the worst word I ever heard! We've got three planets and seven moons that we can think of as "us" and now all of a sudden —' She clamped her jaws shut morosely.

'May I tell you something?'

'Yes.' Maren nodded.

He said huskily, 'My first impulse. Was. To jump.'

'You're airborne? In a hopper?'

He nodded, unable to speak.

'Okay. Fly here to Paris. So it costs. Pay! Just get here and then you and I together —'

Lars said, 'I'd never make it.' I'd jump somewhere along the way, he realized. And he saw, she realized it too.

Levelly, with that great female earth-mother coolness of conduct, that supernatural balance that a woman could draw on when she had to, Maren said, 'Now look, Lars. Listen. You're listening?'

'Yep.'

'Land.'

'Okay.'

'Who's your doctor? Outside of Todt?'

'Got no doctor outside of Todt.'

'Lawyer?'

'Bill Sawyer. You know him. That guy with a head like a hardboiled egg. Only the color of lead.'

Maren said, 'Fine. You land at his office. Have him draw up what's called a writ of mandamus.'

'I don't get it.' He felt like a small boy with her again, obedient but confused. Faced by facts beyond his little ability.

'The writ of mandamus is to be directed at the Board.' Maren said. 'It shall require them to permit you to sit with them in session. That is your goddam legal right, Lars. I mean it. You have a legal, God-given right to walk in there to that conference room down in the *kremlin* and take your seat and participate in everything that's decided.'

'But,' he said hoarsely, 'I've got nothing to offer them: I have nothing. Nothing!' He appealed to her, gesturing.

'You're still entitled to be present,' Maren said. 'I'm not worried about that dung-ball in the sky; I'm worried about *you*.' And, to his astonishment, she began to cry.

TWELVE

Three hours later – it had taken his attorney that long to get a judge of the Superior Court to sign the writ – he boarded a pneumatic-tube null-lapse train and shot from New York down the coast to Festung, Washington, D.C. The trip took eighty seconds, including braking-time.

The next he knew he was in downtown Pennsylvania Avenue surface traffic, moving at an abalone's pace toward the dinky, transcendentally modest above-surface edifice which acted as an entrance to the authentic subsurface *kremlin* of Festung, Washington, D.C.

At five-thirty p.m. he stood with Dr. Todt before a neat young Air Arm officer, who held a laser rifle, and silently presented his writ.

It took a little time. The writ had to be read, studied, certified, initialed by a sequence of office-holders left over from Harding's administration. But at last he found himself with Dr. Todt descending by silent, hydraulic elevator to the subsurface, the *very* subsurface, levels below.

With them in the elevator was a captain from the Army, who looked wan and tense. 'How'd you make it in here?' the captain asked him; evidently he was a dispatch-runner or some such fool thing. 'How'd you get by all that security fnug?'

Lars said, 'I lied.'

There was no more conversation.

The elevator doors opened; the three of them exited. Lars –

with Dr. Todt, who had been silent throughout the entire trip and ordeal of presenting the writ – walked and walked until they reached the last and most elaborate security barrier which sealed off the UN-W Natsec Board, in session within its chambers.

The weapon which here and now pointed directly at him and Dr. Todt came, he realized with pride, from a design emanating from Mr. Lars, Incorporated. Through a meager slot in the transparent but impenetrable ceiling-to-floor bulkhead he presented all his documents. On the far side a civilian official, grizzled, bent with canny experience, with even wisdom engraved on his raptor-like features, inspected Lars' identpapers and the writ. He pondered for an excessive time ... but perhaps it was not excessive. Who could say, in a situation like this?

By means of a wall speaker the ancient, efficient official said, 'You may go in, Mr. Powderdry. But the person with you can't.'

'My doctor,' Lars said.

The grizzled old official said, 'I don't care if he's your mother.' The bulkhead parted, leaving an opening just wide enough for Lars to squeeze through; at once an alarm bell clanged. 'You're armed,' the old official said philosophically and held out his hand. 'Let me have it.'

From his pockets Lars brought every object out for inspection. 'No arms,' he said. 'Keys, ballpoint pen, coins. See?'

'Leave everything there.' The old official pointed. Lars saw a window open in the wall. Through it a hard-eyed female clerk was extending a small wire basket.

Into the basket he dumped the entire contents of his pockets and then, upon instruction, his belt with its metal buckle, and last of all, dreamlike, he thought, his shoes. In his stocking feet he padded on to the big chamber room and, without Dr. Todt, opened the door and entered.

At the table General Nitz's chief aide, Mike Dowbrowsky, also a general, but three-star, glanced up at him. Expressionlessly he nodded in greeting and pointed – peremptorily – at a seat vacant beside him. Lars padded over and noiselessly accepted the seat. The discussion continued with no pause, no acknowledgement of his entrance.

An akprop man – Gene Something – had the floor. He was on his stocking feet, gesticulating and talking in a high-pitched squeak. Lars put on an expression of solemn attention, but in reality he simply felt tired. He was, within himself, resting. He had gotten in. What happened now appeared to him an anticlimax.

'Here is Mr. Lars,' General Nitz interrupted Gene Something, all at once, startling Lars. He sat up at once, keeping himself from visibly jerking.

'I got here as quickly as I could,' he said stupidly.

General Nitz said, 'Mr. Lars, we told the Russians that we knew they were lying. That they put BX-3, our code for the new sat, up there. That they had violated section ten of the Plowshare Protocols of 2002. That within one hour, if they did not acknowledge having launched it into its orbit, we intended to release a g-to-a mis and knock it down.'

There was silence. General Nitz seemed to be waiting for Lars to say something. So Lars said, 'And what did the Soviet Government reply?'

'They replied,' General Mike Dowbrowsky said, 'that they would be happy to turn over their own tracking-stations' data on the sat, so that our missile could get an exact fit on it. And they have done so. In fact they supplied additional material, spontaneously, as to a warping field which their instruments had detected and ours had not, a distortion surrounding BX-3, kept there evidently for the purpose of misleading a thermotropic missile.'

'I thought you sent up a team of robot weapon percept-extensors,' Lars said.

After a pause General Nitz said, 'If you live to be a hundred, Lars, you will say, to everyone you ever meet, including me, that there was no team of robot percept-extensors sent up. And, that since this is the case, the fabrication that this "team" was vaporized is the invention of rancid homeopape reporters. Or if that doesn't do it, the deliberate, sensation-
80

mongering invention of that TV personality – what's his name?'

'Lucky Bagman,' said Molly Neumann, one of the con-comodies.

'That a creature like Bagman would naturally dream it up to keep his audience deluded into believing he has a conduit to Festung W, here.' He added, 'Which he doesn't. Whether they like it or not.'

After a pause Lars said, 'What now, general?'

'What now?' General Nitz clapped his hands together before him atop the pile of memoranda, microdocs, reports, abstracts ribbon-style that covered his share of the great table. 'Well, Lars —'

He glanced up, the weary carrot-like face corrupted with utterly unforeseen, unimaginable, feckless amusement.

'As strange as it may sound, Lars, somebody in this room, somebody a bona fide participant of this meeting, actually suggested – you'll laugh – suggested we try to get you to go into one of your song-and-dance acts, you know, with the banjo and blackface, your —' the carrot-like features writhed – 'trances. Can you obtain a weapon from hyper-dimensional space, Lars? Honestly, now. Can you get us something to take out BX-3? Now, Lars, please don't pull my leg. Just quietly say no and we won't vote you out of here; we'll just quietly go on and try to think of something else.'

Lars said, 'No, I can't.'

For a moment General Nitz's eyes flickered; it was, possibly but not very probably, compassion.

Whatever it was, it lasted only an instant. Then the sardonic glaze reinstated itself. 'Anyhow you're honest, which is what I asked for. Ask for a *no* answer, get a *no* answer.' He laughed barkingly.

'He could try,' a woman named Min Dosker said in an oddly high, lady-like voice.

'Yes,' Lars agreed, taking the bit before General Nitz could seize it and run with it. 'Let me clarify. I —'

'Don't clarify,' General Nitz said slowly. 'Please, as a favor to me personally. Mrs. Dosker, Lars, is from SeRKeb. I failed to tell you, but —' He shrugged. 'So, in view of that fact, don't treat us to an interminable recitation of how you can operate and what you can and can't do. We're not being *entirely* candid because of Mrs. Dosker's presence here.' To the SeRKeb rep, General Nitz said, 'You understand, don't you, Min?'

'I still think,' Mrs. Dosker said, 'that your weapons medium could try.' She rattled her micro-docs irritably.

'What about yours?' General Dowbrowsky demanded. 'The Topchev girl?'

'I am informed,' Mrs. Dosker said, 'that she is —' She hesitated; obviously, she, too, was constrained to be to some extent reticent.

'Dead,' General Nitz grated.

'Oh no!' Mrs. Dosker said, and looked horrified, like a Baptist Sunday school teacher shocked by an improper word.

'The strain probably killed her,' Nitz said lazily.

'No. Miss Topchev is – in shock. She fully understands the situation, however. She is under sedation at the Pavlov Institute at New Moscow, and for the time being she can't work. But she's not *dead*.'

'When?' one of the concomodies, a male nullity, asked her. 'Will she be out of shock soon? Can you predict?'

'Within hours, we hope,' Mrs. Dosker said emphatically.

'All right,' General Nitz said, in a sudden brisk voice; he rubbed his hands together, grimaced, showing his yellow, irregular, natural teeth. Speaking to Lars he said, 'Powderdry, Mr. Lars, Lars, whatever you are – I'm glad you came here. I truly am. I knew you would. People like you can't stand being hung-up on.'

'What kind of person —' Lars began, but General Bronstein, seated on the far side of General Dowbrowsky, shot him a look that made him cease – and God forbid, flush. General Nitz said, 'When were you last at Fairfax, Iceland?'

'Six years ago,' Lars said.

'Before that?'

'Never.'

'You want to go there?'

'I'd go anywhere. I'd go to God. Yes, I'll be glad to go.'

'Fine.' General Nitz nodded. 'She ought to be out of shock by, say, midnight Washington time. Right, Mrs. Dosker?'

'I'm positive,' the SeRKeb rep said, her head wobbling up and down like a vast, colorless pumpkin on its thick stalk.

'Ever tried working with another weapons medium?' an akprop – it would be an akprop – man asked Lars.

'No.' Happily, he was able to keep his voice steady. 'But I'll be pleased to pool my ability and years of experience with Miss Topchev's. As a matter of fact —' He hesitated until he could find a political way of finishing his utterance. 'I've speculated for some time that such a merger might be highly profitable for both blocs.'

General Nitz said, deliberately offhandedly, 'We have this psychiatrist at Wallingford Clinic. There are currently three new, proposed weapons media – is that the proper plural? No – who are relatively untested but whom we *could* draw on.' To Lars he said with abrupt bluntness, 'You wouldn't like that, Mr. Lars; you wouldn't want that at all. So we'll spare you that. For the time being.'

With his right hand General Nitz made a tic-like gesture. At the far end of the chamber, a youthful U.S. commissioned officer bent and clicked on a vidset. Speaking into an ingrafted throat microphone, the officer conferred with persons not present in the room; then, straightening, he pointed to the vidset, indicating that now it – whatever it was – could be considered ready.

On the vidset formed a face, a mystifying source of human essence, wavering slightly in indication that the signal was being relayed from a quite distant spot via a satellite.

Pointing at Lars, General Nitz said, 'Can our boy put his head together with your girl?'

On the vidscreen the far-distant eyes of the wavering face scrutinized Lars, while at his microphone the young officer translated.

'No,' the face on the screen said.

'Why not, Marshal?' Nitz said.

It was the face of Peep-East's highest dignitary and holder of power, the Chairman of the Central Committee of the

Communist Party as well as Secretary of the SeRKeb. The man on the screen, deciding against the fusion, was the Soviet Marshal of the Red Army. Maxim Paponovich. And that man, overruling every other living person in the world on this matter, said, 'We must keep her from the publicity. She is poorly. You know; sick? I regret. It is a shame.' And, cat-like, Paponovich, with smoldering eyes, surveyed Lars for his reaction as if reading him out of a well-broken, long known code.

Rising respectfully to his feet, Lars said, 'Marshal Paponovich, you're making a dreadful error. Miss Topchev and I can be looked to for redress. Is the Soviet Union opposed to the search for remedy in this bad situation?'

The face, tangibly hating him, continued to confront him from the screen.

'If I'm not permitted to cooperate with Miss Topchev,' Lars said, 'I will shore up the security of Wes-bloc and call it quits. I'm asking you now to change your mind, for the protection of the billions of people of Peep-East. And I'm prepared to make public the nature of our attempt to compile our separate talents, despite what this formal Board may instruct. I have direct access to informedia such as the Lucky Bagman interviewers. And your refusal —'

'Yes,' Marshal Paponovich said. 'Miss Topchev will be at Fairfax, Iceland, within the next twenty-four hours.' And the look of his face said: You made us do only what we *intended* to do. And you have taken all of the responsibility so that if it fails it is on you – So we have won. Thank you.

'Thank *you*, Marshal,' Lars said, and reseated himself. He did not give a damn whether or not he had been skillfully manipulated. What mattered was that within the next twenty-four hours he would meet Lilo Topchev at last.

were undoubtedly deposited from ships. Dropped out like eggs, not launched and then halted at orbital plane. Nobody saw any ships. No monitors caught anything. Anti-matter alien inter-system vessels. And always we thought —'

'We thought,' Lars said, 'that sub-epidermal fungiforms from Titan that knew how to simulate everyday household objects shapewise were our great unTerran adversary. Something that looked like a vase and then when you had your back turned seeped into your dermal wall and migrated to the omentum where it resided until surgically cut out.'

'Yes,' Kaminsky agreed. 'I hated those; I saw one once, not in object-simulation but in cyst form, like you depict. Ready for cobalt-bombardment.' He looked physically very sick. 'But Mr. Lars, doesn't that tell us? We know the possibilities. I mean rather we know we *don't* know.'

'No percept-extensors have picked up any clues as to the morphology of these —' the only word he had heard so far was *alien* – 'these adversaries,' he finished.

Kaminsky said, 'Please, Mr. Lars. You and I can take time to talk about easy things. What did you want, sir? Not to hear the bad news. Something else. Anything.' He poured himself cold, dark tea.

'I'm to meet with Lilo Topchev in Fairfax as soon as she's psychologically fit. That time back there in the coffee shop you asked me about a component on them —'

'No deal is needed. I forget weapons item. We are not plowsharing now, Mr. Lars. We will never plowshare again.'

Lars grunted like an animal.

'Yes,' Kaminsky said. 'Never again. You and I – not individual you and I but ethnological totalities, East, West – rose from savagery and waste; we were smart; we became buddy-buddies, made deals, you know, hand-clasp on it, our words in the Protocols of '02. We went back to being, what does the Jewish Christian Bible say? Without leaves.'

'Naked,' Lars said.

'And now plain jane in the streets,' Kaminsky said, 'or what do you call him? Poor sap. Poor sap reads in homeopape about two new not-us kind of satellite and he maybe worries a little;

says, Wonder which modern new weapons work the best on this apparition. This weapon? No? Then that. Or that.' Kaminsky gestured at nonexistent weapons that might have thronged his small office; bitterness made his voice into a wail. 'On Thursday, first They-satellite. Friday, second They-satellite. So on Saturday —'

'On Saturday,' Lars said, 'we use weapons catalog item 241 and the war is over.'

'241.' Kaminsky chuckled. 'A bell rings, thank you. For use exclusively against exoskeleton life forms, dissolves chitinous substances and makes – poached egg, right? Yes, poor sap would enjoy that. I recall KACH-people's pirated video tape of 241 in dramatic action. Good thing you could locate chitinous life form on Callisto to humble; otherwise graphic demonstration would not have been effective. Even I was moved. Down there below California, in Lanferman's catacombs. Must be thrilling to observe creative processes in different states. Right?'

'Right,' Lars said stolidly.

From his desk Kaminsky selected a Xeroxed document, one-page only, for this day and age it was an anomaly. 'This is poop-sheet, for we to give here at Soviet Embassy to news media of Wes-bloc. *Not* official, you understand. A "leak." Homeopape and TV interviewers "overhear" discussion and get general notion of what Peep-East plans, and so forth.' He tossed the document to Lars.

Picking it up Lars saw at a glance the strategy of SeRKeb.

Amazing, Lars thought as he read the one-page Xeroxed copy of the Peep-East document. They didn't mind behaving idiotically; they just wanted to protect themselves from having this idiocy noised about. And right now. Not after the aliens are routed, he realized, or we succumb to them; whatever ultimately happens. Paponovich, Nitz and the nameless second-string are scribbling busily not merely to protect four billion humans from a superlative menace that hangs – literally – over our heads but to get their own damn bastard rascally selves off the hook.

The vanity of man. Even in the highest places.

To Kaminsky he said, 'I glean from this document a new theory about God and the Creation.'

Nodding, Kaminsky politely, waxenly, waited to hear.

Lars said, 'I all of a sudden understand the whole story of the Fall of Man. Why things went wrong. It's one great White Paper.'

'You are wise, Mr. Lars,' Kaminsky said, with weary appreciation. 'I agree; we know, don't we? The Creator bungled and rather than correcting bungle He concocted cover-story which proved someone else responsible. A mythical nogoodnik who *wanted* it this way.'

'So a minute sub-contractor in the Caucasus,' Lars said, 'is going to lose his government contract and be sued. The director of this autofact – and I can't pronounce his name or the fac's – is going to discover something he didn't know.'

'He knows now,' Kaminsky said. 'Now tell me. Why are you here at the embassy?'

'I wanted to get a good pic, three-D and in color, possibly even animated, if you have it, of Miss Topchev.'

'Of course. But you can't wait a day?'

'I want to be prepared in advance.'

'Why?' Kaminsky's eyes were sharp with old acuity.

Lars said. 'You never heard of bridal portraits.'

'Ah. Plot of many plays, operas, heroic legend; done to death, ought to be buried forever. You're serious, Mr. Lars? Then you've got troubles. What is called here in your Wesblock *problems*.'

'I know.'

'Miss Topchev is wrinkled, dried-out, leather-like handbag. Should be in old folks' home, except for the medium talent.'

The blow almost unhinged him; he felt himself calcify.

'You croaked just now,' Kaminsky said. 'Sorry, Mr. Lars. Psychological experiment Pavlov style. I regret it and apologize. Consider. You are going to Fairfax to save four billion. Not to find mistress to replace Maren Faine, your *Liebesnacht* compatriot of the moment. As you found her to replace – what was her name? Betty? The one before, the one KACH says had lovely legs.'

'Christ,' Lars said. 'Always that KACH. Living things turned into data sold by the inch.'

'To any buyer, too,' Kaminsky reminded him. 'To your enemy, your friend, wife, employer, or worse: employees. The agency on which blackmail grows like mold. But as you discovered in that blurred pic of Miss Topchev, something always is held back. To keep you dangling. To make sure you still need more, yet. Look, Mr. Lars; I have a family, wife and three children in Soviet Union. Two They-satellites in our sky, they can kill so as to get at me. They can get at you, maybe if your mistress in Paris died in some awful way, contaminated or infused or —'

'Okay.'

'I just want to petition you; that's all. You will be in Fairfax to see that nothing happens like that to us. I pray to God you and Lilo Topchev imagine up some masterpiece that will be a shield; we are children, playing under the protection of a father's armor. See? If you forget that —'

Kaminsky produced a key, unlocked an old-fashioned drawer of his desk. 'I own this. Dated.' It was an explosion-pellet automatic that he held up, its muzzle pointed carefully away from Lars. 'As an official in an organization that can never back down but would have to be burned out, destroyed, for it to cease, I can offer you an advanced piece of news. Before you leave for Fairfax you will be told there is no returning. Somewhere we make a mistake. A picket ship or immense-radius-orbit monitoring satellite, a solar-sat, failed. And because of it maybe a relay system or a percept-extensor did nothing.' He shrugged, put the automatic hand-weapon away in the desk drawer, scrupulously relocking it with his key. 'I am ranting.'

Lars said, 'You should see a psychiatrist while you're still stationed in Wes-bloc.' Turning, he left Kaminsky's office. He pushed the door open and emerged in the buzzing, activity-drenched main chambers.

Following after him, Kaminsky halted at the office door and said, 'I would do it myself.'

'Do what?' He turned, briefly.

'With what I showed you, locked in the desk.'

'Oh.' Lars nodded. 'Okay. I've got that noted.'

Thereupon he numbly made his way among the scurrying minor bureaucrats of the embassy, through the front door, and out onto the sidewalk.

They're out of their minds, he said to himself. They still believe that in a really tight situation, when it really matters, things can be solved that way. Their evolution of the last fifty years has been all on the surface. Underneath they remain the same.

So not only do we face the presence of two alien satellites orbiting our world, Lars realized, but we have to endure, under this not-prepared-for stress, a return to the unsheathed sword of the past. So all the covenants and pacts and treaties, the locker at the Greyhound bus station at Topeka, Kansas, Geldthaler Gemeinschaft in Berlin, Fairfax itself – it's a delusion. And we both, East and West, shared it together. It's as much our fault as theirs, the willingness to believe and take the soft road out. Look at me now, he thought. In this crisis I've headed straight for the Soviet Embassy.

And look what it got me. An automatic old-time hand-weapon pointed, in the service of the technical aspects of bodily safety, at the roof instead of my abdominal cavity.

But that man was right. Kaminsky was telling me the truth, not blustering or engaging in hysteria. If Lilo and I fail, we will be destroyed. The blocs will then turn elsewhere for assistance. The heavy burden will fall on Jack Lanferman and his engineers, most especially Pete Freid – and God help them if they can't do it either, because if so then they will follow Lilo and me into the grave.

Grave, he thought, you were once asked where your victory is. I can point it out for you. It is here. Me.

As he hailed a passing hopper car he realized suddenly. And I didn't even get what I went into that building for; I couldn't wangle a clear pic of Lilo.

In that, too, Kaminsky had been correct. Lars Powderdry would have to wait until the meeting at Fairfax. He would *not* go in prepared.

FOURTEEN

Late that night, as he lay sleeping in his New York conapt, *they* came.

'She's all right now, Mr. Lars. So do you want to throw your clothes on? We'll pack the rest for you and send it later. We'll go directly up to the roof. Our ship is there.' The leader of the FBI men or CIA men or God knew what kind of men, anyhow professionals and accustomed to being awake and at their duties at this time of night, began, to Lars' incredulity, to rummage in his dresser drawers and closets, gathering his clothes in an efficient, silent, machine-at-work encirclement, they were all around him, doing what they had been sent for. He stood in sleepy, animal-irritable, benumbed bewilderment.

But out of this, full wakefulness at last came, and he padded to the bathroom.

As he washed his face, one of the police in the other room said to him casually, 'They've got three up, now.'

'Three,' he said, moronically, confronting his sleep-squeezed, wrinkled face in the mirror. His hair hung like dry seaweed over his forehead and he automatically reached for a comb.

'Three satellites. And this third one is different, or so the tracking-stations say.'

Lars said, 'Hedgehog?'

'No, just different. It's not a monitoring rig. It's not gathering info. The first two were; now maybe they've done their job.'

'They've proved,' Lars said, 'by being able to remain up there, that we can't bring them down.' No mass of sophisticated equipment jammed into the two sats was necessary to establish *that*; they might as well be hollow.

The police wore commonplace gray-eminence style cloaks

and looked, with their close-shaven heads, like excessively ascetic monks. They ascended to the roof of the conapt building. The man on Lars' right, rather ruddy of complexion, said, 'We understand you visited the Soviet Embassy this afternoon.'

'That's right,' Lars said.

'That writ you have —'

'It just forbids them to accost me,' he said. 'I can accost them. They don't have a writ.'

The policeman said, 'Any luck?'

That did stump him. He pondered in silence, unable to answer. Did the query mean that these FBI or CIA people knew why he had gone to Kaminsky? At last, as they crossed the roof-field to the parked government ship, of a familiar, pursuit-class, great-cruising-range style, Lars said, 'Well, he made *his* point. If you call that "luck." '

The ship rose. New York rapidly fell behind; they were out over the Atlantic. Lights, the habitations of man far below, dwindled and were lost to sight. Lars, peering back, felt an anxious, perhaps even neurotic regret; he experienced a sense of acute, pervasive loss. A loss which could never be compensated for, throughout all eternity.

'How are you going to act?' asked the policeman at the controls.

'I will give the absolute, total, entire, exhaustive, holistic, unconditional impression,' Lars said, 'that I am being candid, naïve, open, honest, truthful, prolix, verbose —'

Sharply the policeman said, 'You stupid bastard – our lives are at stake!'

Lars said somberly, 'You're a cog.'

The policeman – both policemen, in fact – nodded.

'Then you know,' Lars said, 'that I can provide you with a gadget, a plowshare component of a sixty-stage guidance-system, which will light your cigars and make up new Mozart string quartets as background while another gadget, a plowshared component from some *other* multiplex item, serves you your food, even chews it for you and if necessary spits any and all seeds out, into a gadget —'

'I can see,' one of the two police said to his companions,

'why they hate these weapons fashion designers so goddam much. They're fairies.'

'No,' Lars said. 'You're wrong; that's not what ails me. You want to know what ails me? How long before we reach Fairfax?'

'Not long,' both policemen said simultaneously.

Lars said, 'I'll do my best. What ails me is this. I'm a failure at my work. And that hurts a man; that makes him fearful. But I'm paid, or have been up to now, to be a failure. That's what was wanted.'

'You think, Powderdry,' the policeman seated beside him said, 'that you and this Lilo Topchev can do it? Before they —' he pointed upward, an almost pious gesture, like that of some ancient tiller of the soil, a job who had been burned and then burned again – 'drop whatever it is they're setting up their sat-network to make the calculations for? So when they do drop it, it'll hit exactly where they want it? Like for instance, and this is my theory, turning the Pacific to steam and boiling us like a lot of Maine lobsters.'

Lars was silent.

'He's not going to say,' the policeman at the controls said in a curiously mixed tone. There was anger in his voice but also grief. It was a small-boy sound, and Lars sympathized with it. He must have sounded like this himself, at times.

Lars said, 'At the Soviet Embassy they told me, and they meant it, that if Lilo and I came up with nothing or with only the pseudo-weps we've all made our livelihoods off for decades now, they would kill me and her. And they will – if you don't first.'

At the controls the policeman said, calmly, 'We will first. Because we'll be closer. But not right away; there'll be a suitable interval.'

'Were you ordered to?' Lars asked, with curiosity. 'Or is this your own idea?'

No answer.

'You can't both kill me,' Lars said, a feeble attempt to be philosophical and flippant. It failed to be the former, and the latter was not appreciated. 'Maybe you can,' he said, then. 'St.

94

Paul says a man can be born again. He can die and return to life. So if a man can be born twice why can't he be assassinated twice?'

'In your case,' the policeman beside him said, 'it wouldn't be assassination.'

He did not elect to specify what it in fact would be. Perhaps, Lars thought, it was unspeakable. He felt the burden of their mingled hatred and fear and yet – their trust. They still had hope, as Kaminsky had. They had paid him for years not to produce a genuinely lethal device and now, with absolute naïvete, they clung to his skirts, begging, as Kaminsky had begged – and yet with the ugly undercurrent of threat, of murder in case he failed.

He began to understand much that he had never realized about cog society.

Being on the inside, knowing the real scoop, had not eased their lives. Like him, they still suffered. They were not puffed-up, prideful, shot full, as someone had said to him recently, with *hubris*. Knowing what was really going on made them uneasy – for the same reason that *not* knowing made the multitude, the pursaps, able to sleep in peace. Too much of a burden, that of maturity, of responsibility, lay on the cogs … even on these nonentities, these two cops, plus their cohorts back at his conapt who were undoubtedly right now stuffing all his cloaks, shirts, shoes and ties and underwear into boxes and suitcases.

And the essence of the burden was this:

They knew, as Lars himself knew, that their destiny lay in the hands of halfwits. It was as simple as that. Halfwits in both East and West, halfwits like Marshal Paponovich and General Nitz … halfwits, he realized, and felt his ears sear and flame red, *like himself*. It was the sheer mortality of the leadership that frightened the ruling circles. The last 'superman,' the final Man of Iron, had been Josef Stalin. Since then – puny mortals, job-holders who made deals.

And yet, the alternative was frightfully worse – and they all, including even the pursaps, knew this on some level.

They were seeing, in the form of three alien satellites in

their sky, that alternative now.

At the controls the cop said, drawlingly, as if it didn't matter quite so much, 'There's Iceland.'

Below them the lights of Fairfax glowed.

FIFTEEN

Lights blazed, creating a golden-white tunnel for him to walk along. The right-to-the-bone wind from the glaciers to the north snapped longingly at him and he walked rapidly, the two police following. They were shivering too, the three of them making for the closest building as fast as possible.

The building's door sealed itself shut after them and warmth surrounded them. They halted, panting, the cops' faces terribly red now and swollen, not so much from the sudden alterations of atmosphere but from tensions, as if they had feared being caught out there and left.

Four members of the KVD, the Soviet Secret Police, in old-fashioned pre-cloak, ultra-unfashionable wool suits and narrow, pointed oxfords and knit ties, appeared from nowhere. It was as if they had literally detached themselves, super-science-wise, from the walls of the antechamber in which Lars and the two Wes-bloc United States police stood panting.

Soundlessly, in a slow, ritualized moment of truth, the Wes-bloc and Soviet secret police exchanged identification. They must have carried, Lars decided, ten pounds of ident-material apiece. The swapping of cards and wallets and cephalic buzz-keys seemed to continue forever.

And no one said anything. No one of the six so much as looked at any of the others. All attention was fastened fixedly on the ident-elements themselves.

He walked off, found a hot-chocolate machine, put in a dime and soon had his paper cup; he stood sipping, feeling tired, conscious that his head ached and that he had not bothered to shave. He felt keenly the substandard, inappropriate and just plain rotten-looking sight that he presented. And at this time. In these circumstances.

When the Wes-bloc police, had concluded their swapping of ident-material with their Peep-East counterparts, he said caustically, 'I feel like a victim of the Gestapo. Rousted out of bed, unshaved and with my worst clothes, having to face —'

'You won't be facing a *Reichsgericht*,' one of the Peep-East police said, overhearing. His English was a trifle artificial in its precision, learned probably from an audio edutape. Lars thought at once of robots, androids and machinery in general; it was not a sanguine omen. Such plateau, toneless palaver, he recalled was often associated with certain subforms of mental illness – in fact with brain-damage in general. Silently he groaned. He knew now what T. S. Eliot meant about the world ending with a whimper instead of a bang. It would end with his inaudible moan of complaint at the mechanical aspect of those who had him – and this was the true nature of his situation, whether he enjoyed facing it or not – in captivity.

Wes-bloc, for reasons which would of course not be handed down to him to fathom or appreciate, was permitting the encounter with Lilo Topchev to take place under the jurisdiction of the Soviet Union. Perhaps it showed how little hope General Nitz and those in his entourage had that anything of worth might arise out of this.

'I'm sorry,' Lars said to the Soviet policeman. 'I don't know any German. You'll have to explain.' Or else take it up with Ol' Orville, back at the apartment. In that other, lost now, world.

The officer said, 'That's right, you Amis speak no foreign languages. But you have an office in Paris. How do you manage?'

'I manage,' Lars said, 'by having a mistress who speaks French, as well as Italian and Russian, and is terrific in bed, all of which you can find noted in your folio on me. She heads my Paris office.' He turned to the two United States police who had brought him here. 'Are you leaving me?'

They answered, with absolutely no sign of guilt or concern, 'Yes, Mr. Lars.' A Greek chorus of abdication from human, moral responsibility. He was appalled. Suppose the Soviets decided not to return him? Where did Wes-bloc turn for its weapons designs from then on? Assuming of course that the investment of Terra's atmosphere by the alien satellites was contained ...

But no one really believed it would be.

That was it. *That* was what had made him expendable.

'Come along, Mr. Lars.' The four Soviet KVB men gathered around him and he found himself escorted up a ramp, across a waiting room in which people – normal, individual, private men and women – sat waiting for transportation or for relatives. Uncanny, he thought; like a dream.

He asked, 'Can I stop and buy a magazine at the newsrack?'

'Certainly.' The four KVB men steered him to the vast display and watched, like sociologists, as he searched for something to read that might please him. The Bible? he thought. Or perhaps I should try the other extreme.

'How about this?' he asked the KVB men, holding up a comic book printed in cheap, lurid colors. '*The Blue Cephalopod Man from Titan.*' As near as he could tell, it was the worst rubbish on sale here at this enormous display counter. With a U.S. coin he paid the automatic clerk, which thanked him in its autonomic, nasal voice.

As the five of them walked on, one of the KVB men asked him, 'You normally read such fare, Mr. Lars?' His tone was polite.

Lars said, 'I have a complete file back to volume one, number one.'

There was no response; just a formal smile.

'It has declined, though,' Lars added. 'During the last year.' He rolled the comic book up, thrust it into his pocket.

Later, as they buzzed above the rooftops of Fairfax in a USSR government military hopper, he unrolled the comic book and pondered it by the dim dome light above his head.

He had of course never examined such garbage before. It was interesting. The Blue Cephalopod Man, in a long and much honored tradition, burst buildings, knocked out crooks, disguised himself at both ends of each episode as Jason St. James, a colorless computer-operator. That, too, was standard, for reasons lost in the obscurity of the history of comic book art, but having somehow to do with Jason St. James' girl friend, Nina Whitecotton, who wrote a gourmet column for the Monrovia *Chronicle-Times*, a mythical homeopape cranked forth for sale throughout West Africa.

Miss Whitecotton, interestingly, was a Negro. And so were all the other humans in the comic strip, including the Blue Cephalopod Man himself when he put on mortality as Jason St. James. And the locale was, throughout each episiode, 'a large metropolitan area somewhere in Ghana.'

The comic book was aimed at an Afro-Asia audience. By some fluke of the world-wide autonomic distributing mechanism, it had shown up here in Iceland.

In the second episode the Blue Cephalopod Man temporarily was drained of his abnormal powers by the presence of a meteor of zularium, a rare metal 'from the Betelgeuse system.' And the electronic device by which the Blue Cephalopod Man's sidekick, Harry North, a physics professor at Leopoldville, restored those lost powers, just in time to nab the monsters from 'Proxima's fourth planet, Agakana,' was a construct astonishingly like his own weapons design item 204.

Strange! Lars continued reading.

In Episode three, the terminal section of the comic book, another machine peculiarly familiar to him – he could not precisely place it, however – was brought into play by the cunning assistance of timely Harry North. The Blue Cephalopod Man triumphed again, this time over things from the sixth planet of Orionus. And a good thing, too, because these particular things were an abomination; the artist had outdone himself.

'You find that interesting?' one of the KVB men inquired.

I find, Lars thought, it interesting inasmuch as the writer and/or illustrator has made use of KACH to pirate a few of my most technologically interesting ideas. I wonder if there are grounds for a civil suit.

However, now was not the time. He put the comic book away.

The hopper landed on a roof; the engine ceased turning and the door was at once held open for him so that he could disemhopper.

'This is a motel,' one of the artificially precise of speech KVB men explained to him. 'Miss Topchev occupies the entire establishment. We have cleared out the other guests and posted security sentries. You will not be disturbed.'

'Really? On the level?'

The KVB man reflected, turning the phrase about in his mind. 'You may call for assistance at any time,' he said at last. 'And of course for maintenance-service such as sandwiches, coffee, liquor.'

'Drugs?'

The KVB man turned his head. Like solemn owls, all four men stared at Lars.

'I'm on drugs,' Lars explained. 'I thought KACH had told you that, God, I take them hourly!'

'What drugs?' The inquiry was cautious, if not downright drenched with suspicion.

Lars said, 'Escalatium.'

That did it. Consternation. 'But Mr. Lars! Escalatium is brain-toxic! You wouldn't live six months!'

'I also take Conjorizine,' Lars said. 'It balances the metabolic toxicity. I mix them together, grind them into a powder with a rounded teaspoon, make the mixture into a water-soluble near precipitate and take it as an injectable —'

'But, sir, you'd die! From motor-vascular convulsions. Within half an hour.' The four Soviet policemen looked appalled.

'All I ever got as a side-effect,' Lars said, 'was post-nasal drip.'

The four KVB men conferred and then one of them said to Lars, 'We will have your Wes-bloc physician, Dr. Todt, flown here. He can supervise your drug-injection procedures.

Ourselves, we can't take responsibility. Is this stimulant-combination essential for your trance-state to happen?'

'Yep.'

Again they conferred. 'Go below,' they instructed him, at last. 'You will join Miss Topchev – who does not to our knowledge rely on drugs. Stay with her until we can produce Dr. Todt and your two medications.'

They glowered at him severely. 'You should have told us or brought the drugs and Dr. Todt with you! The Wes-bloc authorities did not inform us.' Clearly, they were sincerely angry.

'Okay,' Lars said, and started toward the down-ramp.

A moment later, accompanied by one of the KVB men, he stood at the door of Lilo Topchev's motel room.

'I'm scared,' he said, aloud.

The KVB man knocked. 'Afraid, Mr. Lars, to pit your talent against that of *our* medium's?' The mocking overtones were enormous.

Lars said, 'No, not that.' Afraid, he thought, that Lilo will be what Kaminsky had said, a blackened, shriveled, dried-up leather-like stick of bones and skin, like a discarded purse. Consumed, perhaps, by her vocational demands. God knows what she may have been forced to give by her 'client.' Because they are much harsher on this side of the world ... as we have known all along.

In fact, he realized, that might explain why General Nitz wanted our joint efforts at weapons design to take place under the administration of Peep-East, not Wes-block authority. Nitz recognizes that more decisive pressures are brought to bear here. He may think that under them I will function better.

In other words, Lars thought dully, that I've been holding back all these years. But here, under KVB jurisdiction, under the eyes of the Soviet Union's highest body, the SeRKeb, it will be different.

General Nitz had more faith in Peep-East's capacities to wrest results from its employees than in his own establishment's. What a queer, bewildering, yet somehow true-ringing last little touch.

And, Lars realized, *I believe it, too.*

Because it's probably actually the case.

The door opened and there stood Lilo Topchev.

She wore a black jersey sweater, slacks and sandals, her hair tied back with a ribbon. She looked, was, no more than seventeen or eighteen. Her figure was that of an adolescent just reaching toward maturity. In one hand she held a cigar and held it wrongly, awkwardly, obviously trying to appear grown-up, to impress him and the KVB man.

Lars said huskily, 'I'm Lars Powderdry.'

Smiling, she held out her hand. It was small, smooth, cool, crushable; it was accepted by him gingerly, with the greatest deference. He felt as if by one unfortunate squeeze he could impair it forever. 'Hi,' she said.

The KVB man bumped him bodily inside the room. And the door shut after him, with the KVB man on the other side.

He was alone with Lilo Topchev. The dream had come to pass.

'How about a beer?' she said. He observed when she spoke that her teeth were exceedingly regular, tiny and even. German-woman-like. Nordic, not Slavic.

'You've got a damn good grasp of English,' he said. 'I wondered how they'd solve the language-barrier.' He had anticipated a deft, self-deprecating, but always present, third-person-on-hand translator. 'Where'd you learn it?' he asked her.

'In school.'

'You're telling the truth? You've never been to Wes-bloc?'

'I've never been out of the Soviet Union before,' Lilo Topchev said. 'In fact most of Peep-East, especially the Sino-dominated regions, are out of bounds to me.' Walking lithely to the kitchen of the more or less cog-class luxurious motel suite to get him the can of beer, she gestured suddenly, attracting his attention. She nodded toward the far wall. And then facing him, her back to the wall, she formed with her lips – but did not say aloud – the word *bug.*

A video-audio system was busily monitoring them. Of course. How could it be otherwise? Here comes the chopper,

102

Lars thought, remembering Orwell's great old classic, *1984*. Only in this case we know we're under scrutiny and, at least theoretically, it's by our good friends. We're *all* friends, now. Except that as Aksel Kaminsky said, and truthfully, if we do not manage to properly jump through the flaming hoop, Lilo and I, our good friends will murder us.

But who can blame them? Orwell missed that point. *They* might be right and we might be wrong.

She brought him the beer.

'Lots of luck,' Lilo said, smiling.

He thought, I'm already in love with you.

Will they kill us, he thought, for that? God help them if so. Because they and their joint civilization, East and West, would not be worth preserving at that price.

'What's this about drugs?' Lilo said. 'I heard you talking with the police outside. Was that true or were you just – you know – making their job difficult?'

Lars said, 'It's true.'

'I couldn't catch the names of the drugs. Even though I had my door open and I was listening.'

'Escalatium.'

'Oh, no!'

'Conjorizine. I mix them together, grind them —'

'I heard that part. You inject them as a mixture; you really do. I thought you just said that for their benefit.' She regarded him with a dignified expression overlain with amusement. It was not disapproval or shock that she felt, nor the moral indignation of the KVB man – who was inevitably simple-minded: that was his nature. With her it was near admiration.

Lars said, 'So I can't do a thing until my physician arrives. All I can do —' he seated himself on a black, wrought-iron chair – 'is drink beer and wait.' And look at you.

'I have drugs.'

'They said otherwise.'

'What they say is as the tunnelling of one worm in one dung heap.' Turning to the audio-video monitor which she had just now pointed out to him she said, 'And that goes for you, Geschenko!'

'Who's that?'

'The KVB surveillance-team Red Army intelligence major who will scan the tape that's being made right now of you and me. Isn't that right, Major?' she said to the concealed monitor.

'You see,' she explained to Lars calmly, 'I'm a convict.'

He stared at her. 'You mean you committed a crime, a legal, specified crime, were tried and —'

'Tried and convicted. All as a pseudo – I don't know what to call it. A mechanism; that's it, a mechanism. By which I am legally at this moment, despite all the political, civil guarantees in the Constitution of the USSR, a person absolutely without recourse. I have no remedy whatsoever through the Soviet courts; no lawyer can get me out. I'm not like you. I *know* about you, Lars, or Mr. Lars. Or Mr. Powderdry, whatever you want to be called. I know how you're set up in Wesbloc. How I've envied over the years your position, your freedom and independence!'

He said, 'You think that I could spit in their eye at any time.'

'Yes. I know it. KACH told me; they got it to me, in spite of the dung-heap inhabitants like Geschenko.'

Lars said, 'KACH lied to you.'

SIXTEEN

She blinked. The dead cigar and the can of beer trembled.

Lars said, 'They have me right now as much as they've had you.'

'Didn't you *volunteer* to come here to Fairfax?'

'Oh, sure!' He nodded. 'In fact I personally talked Marshal

104

Paponovich into the idea. Nobody made me come here; nobody put a pistol to my head. But somebody brought a pistol out of a desk drawer and let me view it, and let me know.'

'An FBI man?' Her eyes were enormous, like those of a little child hearing the exploits of the fabulous.

'No, not an FBI man, technically. A *friend* of the FBI, in this friendly, cooperative world in which we live. It's not important; we don't have to depress ourselves into talking about this. Except that you ought to know that they could have gotten to me any time. And when it mattered they let me know it.'

'So,' Lilo said thoughtfully, 'you haven't been that different. I heard you were a prima donna.'

Lars said, 'I am, I'm difficult. I'm undependable. But they can still get out of me what they want. What else matters?'

'I guess nothing else,' she said, dutifully.

'What drugs do you take?'

'Formophane.'

'It sounds like a new make of one-way mirror.' He had never heard of it. 'Or a plastic milk carton that opens itself and pours itself on your cereal without spilling a drop.'

Lilo said, between gulps, awkward and adolescent, at her can of beer. 'Formophane is rare. You don't have it in the West. It's made by a firm in East Germany that descends from some ancient pre-Nazi pharmaceutical cartel. In fact it's made —' She paused. Obviously she was considering whether it was wise to finish. 'They make it expressly for me,' she said, at last.

There, it was done; she had told him. 'The Pavlov Institute at New Moscow made a six-month analysis of my brain-metabolism to see what could be done to – *improve* it. They came up with this chemical formula and it was Xeroxed and passed on to A. G. Chemie. And A. G. Chemie produces sixty half-grain tablets of Formophane for me a month.'

'And it does what?'

Lilo said, carefully, 'I don't know.'

He felt fear. For her. For what they had done – and could do again any time they wanted. 'Don't you notice any effects?'

he asked. 'Deeper involvement in the trance-state? Longer? Less after-effects? You must notice something. Improvement in your sketches – it must be they give it to you to improve your sketches.'

Lilo said, 'Or to keep me from dying.'

The fear inside him became acute. 'Why dying? Explain.' He kept his voice low, free of affect; it appeared as casual. 'Even considering the quasi-epileptoid nature of —'

'I am a very sick person,' Lilo said. 'Mentally. I have what they call "depressions." They're not depressions and *they* know it; that's why I spent – always will spend – a lot of time at the Pavlov Institute. It's hard to keep me going, Lars. That's the simple fact. It's a day by day proposition, and Formophane helps. I take it. I'm glad to get it – I don't like the "depressions" or whatever they are. You know what they are?' She leaned toward him urgently. 'Want to know?'

'Sure.'

'I watched my hand once. It shriveled up and died and became a corpse hand. It rotted away to dust. And then it became all of me; I no longer lived. And then – I lived again. In another way, the life that's to follow. After I die ... Say something.' She waited.

'Well, that ought to interest the established religious institutions.' It was all he could think of, for the moment.

Lilo said, 'Do you think, Lars, we, the two of us, can do what they want? Can we come up with what they call a "zap gun"? You know. A – I hate to say it – a *real* weapon?'

'Sure.'

'From where?'

'From the place we – visit. As if we took psilocybin. Which is related, as you know, to the adrenal hormone epinephrine. But I always have liked to think of it as if we're taking *teonanacatyl*.'

'What's that?'

'An Aztec word. It means "god's flesh".' He explained. 'You know it under the name of its alkaloid. Mescaline.'

'Do you and I visit the same place?'

'Probably.'

106

'And it's where, did you say?' She cocked her head, waiting, listening, watching. 'You didn't say. You don't know! I know.'

'Then tell me.'

Lilo said, 'I will if you'll take Formophane first.' Rising, she disappeared into the other room. When she returned she carried two white tablets, which she held out to him.

For reasons which he did not know – which really frankly did not interest him – he obligingly, without even verbal protest, drank down the two tablets with his beer. The tablets caught in his throat momentarily. They seemed to stick there, and then were past the point from which they could be coughed forth, expelled. The drug was now a part of him. For whatever it foreboded; for whatever claim the chemical could make on his system – he had taken it on trust. And that was that.

Trust, he realized, not in the drug but in Lilo Topchev.

Lilo said, to his jolted surprise, 'Anyone who would do that, is – a person who has failed.' She seemed sad and yet not disappointed. It was as if his trust had reinforced some deep, instinctual pessimism in her. Or was it something more? The Slavic fatalism?

He had to laugh; he was caricaturizing her. Whereas in fact he knew nothing about her yet, could not at this point decipher her in the least. 'You're going to die,' Lilo said. 'I've been waiting to do this; I'm afraid of you.' She smiled. 'They always told me that if I ever let them down the KVB hatchet-men operating in Wes-bloc would 'nap you, bring you to Bulganingrad and use you, and I'd be discarded on what they call the "rubbish-heap of history." In the old-fashioned way. The way Stalin used."

He said, 'I don't believe for even one second that you're telling me the truth.'

'You don't think you came all the way here just to be assassinated by me.'

He nodded.

After a pause Lilo sighed. 'You're right.'

He sagged with relief; his breathing resumed.

'I *am* afraid of you,' she continued. 'They did threaten me, held you over my head perpetually I got so I hated just *thinking* about you. And I suppose you are going to die. Everybody else does. Everybody else has in the past up to now. But not from what I just now gave you. That was a brain-metabolism stimulant resembling serotonin; it was exactly what I said and I gave it to you because I'm terribly interested to see its effects on you. You know what I want to do? Try your two drugs along with mine. We won't just combine our talent. We'll combine our metabolic stimulants too and see what we get. Because —' she hesitated childishly, openly somber but excited – 'we have to be a success, Lars. We just have to.'

He said reassuringly, 'We will be.'

And then, as he sat there with his beer can in his hand – he was studying it idly, noticing that it was a Danish beer, dark, a very good sort – he felt the drug affect him.

All at once, with a terrible rush like bad fire, it overwhelmed him, and he got stumblingly to his feet, reaching out – the beer can fell, rolled away, its contents staining the rug, dark, ugly, foaming, as if some big animal had been slaughtered helplessly here and its life was draining away. As if, he thought, I have strode into death, despite what she said. God in heaven! I've cut myself open in an effort to – *obey*.

What am I obeying? he asked. Death can dissemble. It can ask for your hide in hidden words and you think it's something entirely else, a high authority, some quality spiritual and free that you ought to enjoy. That's all you ask; you want to be pleased. And instead – it has you. Not *they* but *it*. They would like a lot but they're not ready to ask for that.

However you have given it gratuitously, jumped the gun. They won't like it. Tyranny has its own rate of flow. To run forward toward it prematurely is no more going to be appreciated than if you tried to creep back out, hung back, wandered off, sought to escape in any other way. Than even if, God forbid, you had stood up on your feet and *fought*.

'What's the matter?' Lilo's voice, distantly.

'Your serotonin,' he said with difficulty, 'got to me. Wrongly. The alcohol, the beer. Maybe. Can you – tell me.' He walked one step, two. 'The bathroom.'

108

She guided him, frightened. He could make that out, the flapping batwings, her genuinely fear-stained face as she led him along.

'Don't worry,' he said. 'I'll —' And then he perished.

The world was gone; he was dead and in a bright, terrible world no man had ever known.

SEVENTEEN

There was a man, almost idol-like, graven in the stone-carved clarity of his facial structure. He was bending by Lars, wearing a smart uniform, including a cluster of vari-colored medals.

He said, 'He's alive now.'

Two medical persons hovered. They wore plain white floor-length smocks. Lars saw institutional, stupendously expensive emergency equipment, great chugging machines with hoses and gauges and self-powered engines, everything in furious operation. The air smelled of ionization – highly positive – and chemicals. He saw a table on which instruments rested, one of which he recognized; it was employed to perform immediate tracheaectasies.

But these Soviet medical people had not had to use it with him. He had come around in time.

The monitor, he realized. Hidden in the wall, grinding continually away its audio and video material. Keeping watch for its own sinister, ulterior purposes. It had witnessed his collapse and because of it help had been summoned, and soon enough to save him.

Getting to the bathroom would not quite have been enough.

To the uniformed, bemedaled, starch-collar and shoulder-boarded Red Army officer he said, 'Major Geschenko?'

'Yes, Mr. Lars.' The officer had become now, in relief, rubbery and pale. 'Your vagus. Something about the medulla and especially the esophagus; I don't properly understand. But it was really exceptionally close, for a minute or two. They would of course at the very last cooled you down and flown you out of here. But —' He gestured.

Lars agreed, 'Close. I felt the nearness.' He made out Lilo Topchev now. She stood huddled at the far wall, not taking her eyes off him.

Lilo said, 'Do you imagine I did it on purpose?'

Her voice was far off and barely audible to him. For a moment he believed it was his imagination and then he realized that she had actually asked that. And he realized the answer. He knew the truth.

But aloud, mostly to protect her, he said, 'An accident.'

'It was,' Lilo said faintly.

'I think we're all aware of that,' Major Geschenko said, with a trace of taut irritation. 'An allergic reaction.'

You believe her? Lars wondered. A man in your business? Or is it that *I'm* not supposed to know?

No sir, he thought; you couldn't be fooled. You're a professional. And even I can tell an accident from the real thing. This was real. She made a try and then she got afraid because it would have been the end of her, too. She must have understood that when she saw the drug actually begin to work, the violence of the somatic response. She is just not an adult, he thought. She couldn't foresee.

But why? he wondered. Fear that I'd replace her? Or fear of another kind entirely.

A much more rational fear.

He said, speaking to Lilo, 'It's the weapon.'

'Yes.' Rigidly she nodded.

He said, 'You thought that it would come. By means of us as they hoped for.'

'It would be too much,' Lilo said.

He comprehended. 'The old days, before the Protocols,' he said. 'When there was no deal. No hoax. When it was the real thing.'

110

'It was returning,' Lilo said in a whisper. 'I felt it as soon as I set eyes on you. Together we'd do it and it'd be done and no one could change that. We in our expanded consciousness where they can't go, even with mescaline-psilocybin-Psilocybe mexicana-Stropharia cubensis-d-lysergic acid diethylamide, everything combined; they can't follow us. And they know it.'

Angrily, Major Geschenko said to her in a loud voice, almost a shout, 'The satellites! *Three!* Do you hear me? And there's going to be a fourth and a fifth and it's the end of us!'

'All right,' she said, with composure. 'I hear. You're undoubtedly right.' She sounded defeated.

To Lars, Major Geschenko said with bitter, sardonic wrath, 'Undoubtedly.' He scrutinized Lars, seeking his reaction.

Lars said with difficulty, 'You never will have to worry about me or my attitude. She's wrong, emotionally. I see that clearly – why you've always kept her under such surveillance. I understand perfectly. From now on I want Dr. Todt —'

'He'll be here in several minutes,' Major Geschenko assured him. 'And he'll be with you constantly, so the opportunity for her to try some other psychotic coup to defend herself against imaginary attack won't be even remotely possible. And if you want, in addition one of our own medical officers can —'

'Todt is enough,' he said, and sat up.

'I hope you're right,' Major Geschenko said. He sounded as if he had grave reservations. 'Anyhow we'll defer to your preferences in this matter.' To Lilo he said, 'You could be arraigned, you know.'

She said nothing.

'I want to take the chance,' Lars said. 'I want to go on working with her. Actually we haven't started. We should, right away; I think the situation insists on it.'

Hands shaking, without a word, Lilo Topchev relit her cigar. Ignoring him, staring fixedly at the match in her hand, she puffed gray smoke.

He knew then that he would not trust her for a long, long time. Nor even understand her.

'Tell me,' he said to Major Geschenko. 'Do you have the authority to ask her to put that cigar out? It makes it hard for me to breathe.'

Two plainclothes KVB men at once stepped toward Lilo.

She dropped the burning cigar to the floor, defiantly.

The room was silent as everyone watched her.

'She'll never pick it up,' Lars said. 'You can wait forever.'

A KVB man stooped, picked up the cigar and ground it out in a nearby ashtray.

Lars said, 'But I will work with you. Do you follow me?' He watched her intently, trying to guess what she was thinking and feeling, but he saw nothing. Even the professionals around him seemed to see no harbinger. She has eluded us, he thought. We will just have to go ahead on this bad basis. And she has our lives at stake in those childish hands.

Jesus, he said to himself. What a mess!

Major Geschenko helped him up. Everyone in the room tried to assist, thwarting one another in a silent-movie routine that at any other time would have struck Lars as funny. The major led him off to one side where the two of them could talk.

Geschenko said, 'You understand why we were able to get to you so soon.'

Lars said, 'She pointed out the aud and vid receptors.'

'And you can see why they were installed.'

'I don't care why they were installed.'

'She will function,' Major Geschenko assured him. 'We know her. At least we've done our best to learn enough in order to predict.'

'You didn't foresee this, though.'

'What we didn't see,' Geschenko said, 'was that a preparation benign to her brain-metabolism would be toxic to yours. And we're puzzled as to how she knew, unless she was guessing.'

'I don't think she was guessing.'

'Is there a pre-cog aspect to you mediums?'

'Maybe,' Lars said. 'Is she ill in the clinical sense?'

'You mean psychologically? No. She's reckless; she's full of hate; she doesn't like us or want to cooperate. But not ill.'

'Try letting her go,' Lars said.

'Go? Go where?'

'Anywhere. Free her. Walk away from her. Leave her. You don't understand, do you?' It was obvious; he was wasting his time. But he tried just a little further. The man he was addressing was not an idiot, not a fanatic. Geschenko was merely firmly gripped in the paws of his environment. 'Do you know what a fugue is?' Lars asked.

'Yes. Flight.'

'Let her run until she's run enough to —' He hesitated.

Mockingly, Geschenko said, with the wisdom of an age not confined to his own, not limited to this Soviet world of his here and now, 'To what, Mr. Lars?'

He waited for an answer.

Lars said doggedly, 'I want to sit down with her and as soon as possible begin the work she and I have to do. In spite of ~~~. It shouldn't be allowed to cause delay because that would encourage the tendencies in her that act toward dissolving the cooperative effort that we have to initiate. So get everyone else out and let me see my doctor.'

Dr. Todt said to Lars, 'I'd like to do a multi-phasic on you now.'

Putting his hand on Todt's shoulder Lars said, 'She and I have to work. We'll run the tests some other time. When I'm back in New York.'

' "De gustibus," ' tall, morose, thin-beaked Dr. Todt said fatalistically, ' "non disputandum est." I think you're insane. They've got the formula for that poison held back so we can't analyze it. Only God Himself knows what it did to you.'

'It didn't kill me and we're going to have to be content with that. Anyhow you keep your eyes open all the time, during our trance-states. And if you have any measuring devices you want to keep hooked up to me —'

'Oh yes. I'll be running an EEG and an EKG continually. But just on you. Not her. They can assume responsibility for her; she's not my patient.' Dr. Todt's tone was envenomed. 'You know what I think?'

Lars said, 'You think I ought to go home.'

'The FBI can get you out of —'

'You have the Escalatium and the Conjorizine spansules?'

'Yes, and thank God you're not going to inject. That's the first rational decision you've made.' Todt handed him two small bulging envelopes.

'I don't dare inject. They might potentiate that damn poison she gave me.' He considered himself warned. It would be a while before he took any more chances with even those drugs whose action he was familiar with. Or *imagined* he was familiar with.

Walking over to Lilo Topchev he stood confronting her; she returned his gaze with poise.

'Well,' he said, by way of an appeasing introduction, 'I suppose you could have given me four of those instead of two. It could be worse.'

'Oh, hell,' she said tragically. 'I give up. There's no way out of this idiotic fusion of our minds, is there? I have to cease being an individual, what little they've left me. Wouldn't you be surprised, Mr. Lars, if *I* put those satellites up there? Through a parapsychological talent no one knows about yet?' She smiled happily. The idea seemed to please her, even if it was a fantasy, patently not true. 'Do I scare you by saying that?'

'Nope.'

'I'll bet I could scare *somebody* by saying that. Gosh, if only I had access to the info-media, the way you have. Maybe you could say it for me; you could quote me.'

Lars said, 'Let's start.'

'If you work in unison with me,' Lilo Topchev said quietly, 'I promise something will happen to you. Don't go on. Please.'

'Now,' he said. 'With Dr. Todt right here.'

'Dr. Dead.'

'Pardon?' He was taken aback.

'That's right,' Dr. Todt said from behind him. 'That's what my name means in German. She's perfectly right.'

'And I see that,' Lilo said, half to herself, in an almost singsong chant. 'I see death. If we go on.'

114

Dr. Todt held a cup of water towards Lars. 'For your medication.'

In ritualistic fashion, as before each trance-state, Lars downed one Escalatium and one Conjorizine. Downed rather than injected. The method differed but the results, he hoped, would be the same.

Watching him narrowly, Dr. Todt said, 'If Formophane, which is essential to her, is toxic to you, acts to suppress your sympathetic nervous-system, you might ask yourself this. "How does the structure of my parapsychological talent differ from hers?" Because this is a high order of evidence that it does. Does in fact radically.'

'You don't think she and I can function together?'

'Probably not,' Dr. Todt said quietly.

'I guess we'll know fairly soon,' Lars said.

Lilo Topchev, detaching herself from her place at the far all, walked toward him and said, 'Yes, I guess we will.'

Her eyes were bright.

EIGHTEEN

When Surley Febbs reached Festung, Washington, D.C. he was astonished to discover that, despite his to-the-last-letter perfect assemblage of identification, he could not get in.

Because of the hostile alien satellites in the sky new security measures, formalities and procedures had taken effect. Those who were already within stayed within. Surley G. Febbs, however, was outside.

And thus he remained.

Seated gloomily in a downtown park, gazing in morose frustration at a group of children playing, Febbs asked him-

115

self, Is this what I came here for? I mean, it's a racket! They notify you you're a concomody and then, when you show up, they ignore you.

It passed comprehension.

And those satellites, that's just an excuse, he realized. The bastards just want to keep a monopoly on their power. Anyone with half an eye who has insight into these matters, who has given long study to the human mind and society as I have, can tell this at a glance.

What I need is a lawyer, he decided. Top legal talent, which I could hire if I wanted to.

Only he did not feel like spending the money right now.

Go to the homeopapes, then? But their pages were full of screaming sensational scare headlines about the satellites. No mass sap cared about anything else, such as human values and what was being done to certain individual citizens. As usual, the ignorant average goof was completely taken in by the trash of the day. Not so Surley G. Febbs. But that still did not get him into the *kremlin* below Festung, Washington, D.C.

An ancient, tottering apparition approached in what appeared to be the much-darned, patched and washed remnants of a military uniform of some sort. It made its way slowly to the bench on which Febbs sat, hesitated, and then creakily lowered itself.

'Afternoon,' the old man said in a rusty squeak. He sighed, coughed, rubbed his wet, liverish lips with the back of his hand.

'Mmmmmm,' Febbs grunted. He did not feel like talking, especially with this tattered scarecrow. Should be in a veterans' home, he said to himself, bothering all the other *jerries* – the worn-out old folks who ought to have been dead a long time ago.

'Look at those kids,' The ancient war veteran gestured and despite himself Febbs looked. ' "Olly, olly, oxen free." Know what that's a corruption of? "All the, all the, outs in free." ' The jerry chuckled. Febbs groaned. 'That goes back before you were born. Games never change. Best game ever invented was Monopoly. Ever play that?'

'Mmmmmm,' Febbs said.

'I got a Monopoly board,' the old war vet said. 'Not with me, but I know where I can lay my hands on it. At the club-house.' Again he pointed; his finger was like a winter tree-stalk. 'Want to play?'

'No,' Febbs said clearly.

'Why not? It's an adult game. I play all the time, like eight hours a day sometimes. I always buy the high-priced property at the end, like Park —'

Febbs said, 'I'm a concomody.'

'What's that?'

'A high official of Wes-bloc.'

'You a military man?'

'Hardly.' Military men! Fatbutts!

'Wes-bloc,' the old veteran said, 'is run by military men.'

'Wes-bloc,' Febbs said, 'is an economic, political gestalt the ultimate responsibility for the effective functioning of which rests on the shoulders of a heterogeneous Board composed of —'

'Now they're playing Snum,' the old veteran said.

'What?'

'Snum. I remember that. Did you know what I was in the Big War?'

'Okay,' Febbs said, and decided it was time to move along. In his present mood – denied his legal right to sit on the UN-W Natsec Board – he was not disposed to hear a prolix account of this senile, feeble, tattered old relic's onetime so-called 'exploits.'

'I was main-man for a T.W.G. Maintenance, but I was in uniform. We were right at the line. Ever see a T.W.G. in action? One of the finest tactical weapons ever invented but always giving trouble in the power-feed assembly. One surge and the whole turret burned out – you probably remember. Or maybe that was before your time. Anyhow, we had to keep the feedback from —'

'Okay, okay,' Febbs said, writhing with irritation; he rose to his feet and started off.

'I got hit by a shatter-cone that tore loose from the sword-

117

valve system,' the old war vet was saying as Febbs departed.

Big War my foot, Febbs said to himself. Some minor rebellion of some colony. Some fracas over in a day. And 'T.W.G.!' God knows what obsolete thrown-away heap of junk *that* was, probably back in the primordial 100 series. They ought to make mandatory the scrapping of the operators along with the weapons; it's a disgrace, an old wreck like that wasting really valuable people's time.

Since he had been driven from the park, he decided to make one more stab at entering the *kremlin*.

Presently he was saying to the guard on duty, 'It's a violation of the Wes-bloc constitution! It's nothing but a kangaroo court that's in session down there without me. Nothing it decides on is legal without my vote. You call your superior, your O.D. You tell him that!'

The sentry stared stonily ahead.

All at once a huge black government hopper hovered overhead, to descend toward the concrete field beyond the guard's station. Instantly the guard whipped out a vid receiver-transmitter, began giving orders.

'Whozat?' Febbs asked, devoured by an ant-army of curiosity.

The hopper landed. And from it stepped – General George Nitz.

'General!' Febbs shrieked; his voice carried past the reinforced barrier controlled by the guard, to the man in uniform who had disemhoppered. 'I'm your compeer! I've got papers that prove I'm a legal rep to the Board, a concomody, and I demand that you use your authority to let me in, or I'm going to file a civil action for tort violation or some goddam such thing! I haven't talked to a lawyer yet, but I mean it, General!' His voice died away as General Nitz continued on and disappeared into the surface structure which was the meager portion of the Festung that stood above ground.

A cold Washington, D.C. wind blew about Febbs' legs. The only sound was the guard's voice as he gave instructions into his vidphone.

'Sheoot,' Febbs said, in despair.

118

A small, dilapidated civilian for-hire type hopper now coasted up to the barrier and halted. From it a middle-aged woman in an old-fashioned grime-colored cloth coat stepped. Approaching the guard she said timidly, but with a certain air of firmness, 'Young man, how do I find the UN-W Natsec Board? My name is Martha Raimes and I'm a newly elected concomody.' She fumbled in her purse for proof of her assertion.

The guard lowered his vidphone and said briefly, 'No one with an AA-class or higher pass is to be admitted, madam. Emergency-sit priority of security rating-ruling in effect as of six a.m. time-zone one-fifty this morning. I'm sorry, madam.' He turned his attention back to his vidset thereupon.

Febbs thoughtfully approached the middle-aged woman.

'Miss, I'm in exactly the same disgraceful position as you are,' he informed her. 'We are being denied our legal prerogatives and I have seriously considered the possibility of major litigation against the parties responsible.'

'Is it those satellites?' Martha Raines asked, mouse-like. But her suspicion was almost equal to his own. 'It must be them. Everyone's busy about them and they don't care about us. I came all the way from Portland, Oregon, and this just is too much for me; I voluntarily relinquished my greeting-card shop – turned it over to my sister-in-law – in order to perform my patriotic task. And now look! They're just not going to admit us – I can *see* that.' She seemed more stunned than angry. 'This is the fifth entrance I've tried at,' she explained to Febbs, glad of a sympathetic audience at last. 'I tried gates C, D and then even E and F, and now here. And every time they say the same. They must be *instructed* to.' She nodded solemnly. It was all abundantly, un-Wes-blocly clear.

'We'll get in,' Febbs said.

'But if every one of these —'

'We'll find the other four new concomodies,' Febbs decided. 'We shall act as a group. They won't dare refuse all of us – it's only by splitting us off from each other that they've been able to lord it over us. I seriously doubt if they'd turn *all six* of us down, because that would be to admit that they're conducting

119

their policy-level sessions in deliberate illegality. And I bet if all six of us marched over to one of those autonomic TV interviewers, like one of Lucky Bagman's, and told it, they'd find time to take off from babbling about those satellites long enough to demand that justice be done!'

In fact Febbs had seen several TV interviewers since he had appeared here at the main gate. All the info-media agencies were on constant alert, these days, for news pertaining to the satellites.

All that remained was to round up the other four concomodies. And even as he and Martha Raines stood here, another civilian for-hire hopper began to descend; within it sat a nervous, frustrated-looking youth and Febbs had the acute intuition that this was an additional newly drafted concomody.

And when we do get in, Febbs declared to himself grimly, we'll make them squirm! We'll tell that fatbutt General George Nitz where to head in to.

He hated General Nitz already ... for having paid no attention to him. Nitz did not know that things were about to change. He would soon have to listen, like that time in the old days when Senator Joe McCarthy, that great American of the last century, had made the fatbutts listen. Joe McCarthy in the 1950s had told them off, and now Surley Febbs and five other typical type citizens, armed with absolute, foolproof ident-papers certifying to their vast status as representing two billion humans, were about to do the same!

As the nervous youth emerged from his hopper, Febbs strode purposefully toward him.

'I'm Surley Febbs,' he said grimly. 'And this lady here is Martha Raines. We're newly drafted concomodies. Are you, sir?'

'Y-yes,' the youth said, swallowing visibly. 'And I tried at Gate E and then at —'

'Never mind,' Febbs said, and felt an upsurge of confidence. He had spotted an autonomic TV interviewer. It was coming this way.

Wrathfully, Febbs walked to meet it, the other new concomodies trailing obediently after him. They seemed glad to fall behind him and let him speak.

They had found their leader.

And Febbs felt himself transformed. He was no longer a man. He was a Spiritual Force.

It felt just fine.

NINETEEN

Lars could discern very little, as he sat across from Lilo, watching her intently while Dr. Todt prowled about keeping an eye on the spill of tapes secreted by the EEG and EKG machines attached to his patient. But he thought, *The promise which this girl made is going to be kept*. Harm will arise somehow from this situation. I feel it already, and I am nothing in this. Already Wes-bloc has those three to replace me. And undoubtedly more mediums exist in the East.

But his enemy, his antagonist, was not Peep-East and its KVB; the Soviet authorities had already proved their keen desire to act in his behalf. They had saved his life. His nemesis sat opposite him, an eighteen-year-old girl who wore a black jersey sweater and sandals and tight slacks, whose hair was pulled back with a ribbon. A girl who in her hatred and fear had, as an introduction, already made her first destructive move in his direction.

But, he thought, you are so goddam physically and sexually, so very amazingly sexually, attractive.

I wonder, he wondered, what you are like under that sweater, without those slacks and barefoot, without even that ribbon. Is there any way we can meet in that dimension? Or would the vid and aud monitoring-systems preclude that? Personally, he thought, I wouldn't care if the whole Red Army cadet academy pored over the tapes. But you'd mind. It would make you hate worse, and not hate just them but me as well.

The medication was beginning to affect him. Soon he would go under, and the next he would know, Dr. Todt would be reviving him and there would be – or would not be – a sketch. The production was automatic, neurologically speaking; it either came or it didn't.

He said to Lilo, 'Do you have a lover?'

Her eyebrows knitted ominously. 'Who cares?'

'It's important.'

Dr. Todt said, 'Lars, your EEG shows that you're —'

'I know,' he said, and had difficulty articulating; his jaw had become numbed. 'Lilo,' he said, 'I have a mistress. She heads my Paris branch. You know what?'

'What?' She continued to glower at him suspiciously.

Lars said, 'I'd give Maren up for you.'

He saw her face smooth. Her delighted laugh filled the room. 'Wonderful! You *mean* it?'

He could only nod; it was past the time when speech remained possible. But Lilo saw the nod and the radiance of her face grew to a golden nimbus. Glory incarnate.

From a wall-speaker a business-like voice said, 'Miss Topchev, you must synchronize your Alpha-wave pattern for the trance-phase to Mr. Lars. Should I send in a doctor?'

'No,' she said quickly. The nimbus faded. 'No one from the Pavlov Institute! I can manage it.' She glided from her chair to kneel beside Lars. She rested her head against his, and some of her radiance seeped back from the physical contact; he felt it as pure warmth.

Dr. Todt said nervously to her. 'Twenty-five seconds and Mr. Lars will be under. Can you manage? Your brain-metabolism stimulant?'

'I took it.' She sounded irritable. 'Can't you leave so that it's just the two of us? I guess not.' She sighed. 'Lars,' she said, 'Mr. Powderdry. You weren't afraid even when you realized you were dying; I saw you and you *knew*. Poor Lars.' She ruffled his hair, clumsily. 'And do you know what? I'll tell *you* something. You keep your mistress in Paris, because she

122

probably loves you, and I don't. Let's see what sort of weapon we can make between us. Our baby.'

Dr. Todt said, 'He can't answer you but he can hear you.'

'What a child for two strangers to pawn,' Lilo said. 'Does my killing you make us friends? Good friends? Bosom. Is that the idiom? Or breast-friends; I like that.' She pressed his head down against the scratchy black wool of her sweater.

All this he felt. This black, soft scratchiness; the rise and fall as she breathed. Separated, he thought, from her by organic fiber and also no doubt by an inner layer of synthetic undergarment and then perhaps one additional layer after that, so there are three layers separating me from what is within, and yet it's only the thickness of a sheet of a bookbond paper from my lips.

Will it always be like this?

'Maybe.' Lilo said softly, 'you can die in this posture, Lars. Like my child. You instead of the sketch. Not our baby but mine.' To Dr. Todt she said, 'I'm slipping under, too. Don't worry; he and I will go together. What'll we do in the non-space-time realm where you can't follow? Can you guess?' She laughed. And again, this time less crudely, rumpled his hair.

'God knows,' Todt's voice came distantly to Lars.

And then he was gone. At once the soft black scratchiness departed. That foremost of all, and first.

But he grabbed to retain it, scrabbling like a beclawed beast; yet, even so, instead of the slim shape of Miss Topchev he found his fingers gripping – grotesquely, and hideously disappointingly – a ballpoint pen.

On the floor lay a scribbled sketch. He was back. It seemed impossible, not to be accepted or believed. Except for the fact of his fright; that made it real.

Dr. Todt, busily glancing at the sketch said, 'Interesting, Lars. It is, by the way, one hour later. You have emerged with a simple design for —' he chuckled, Dr. Dead chuckling – 'a donkey-type steam engine.'

Sitting up groggily, Lars picked the sketch from the floor. He saw to his dulled incredulity that Dr. Todt was not joking.

A simple, ancient steam donkey-engine. It was too funny even to try to laugh over.

But that was not all.

Lilo Topchev was crumpled into a heap – like a completed but for reasons unknown discarded android – and one which had been dropped, too, from some immense height. She clutched a wadded sheet of paper. On it was another sketch and this, he saw instantly, even in his semiconscious state, was not any archaic contraption. He had failed but Lilo had not.

He took the sketch from her stiff fingers. She was still quite flown.

'God,' Lilo said distinctly. 'Do I have a headache!' She did not move or even open her eyes. 'What's the result? Yes? No? Just something to plowshare?' She waited, eyes squeezed shut. 'Please, somebody answer me.'

Lars saw that the sketch was not hers. It was his, too, or at least partly his. Some of the lines were unnatural to him – he recognized them from the material which KACH had shown him over the years. Lilo had done part of this and he had done the rest; they had manipulated the writing-stylus in unison. Had they actually gripped it simultaneously? Dr. Todt would know. So would the Soviet big-shots who scanned the vid and aud tape-tracks, and later so would the FBI when these were transmitted to them ... or perhaps even an arrangement had been made to provide both intelligence agencies with the result at one exact synchronized instant.

'Lilo,' he said, 'get up.'

She opened her eyes, raised her head. Her face was haggard, wild, hewn hawk-like.

'You look awful,' he said.

'I am awful. I'm a criminal; didn't I tell you?' She staggered to her feet, stumbled and half-fell; expressionless, Dr. Todt caught her, 'Thank you, Dr. Dead,' she said. 'Did KACH tell you that I'm as a rule sick at my stomach after a trance-phase? Dr. Dead take me into the bathroom. Quick. And phenothiazine; do you have some?' She tottered away. Todt assisting her.

Lars remained seated on the floor with the two sketches.

One of a steam-driven donkey-engine. The other —

It looked, he thought, like an autonomic, homeostatic, thermotropic wise rat catching-device. Only for rats with an IQ of 230 or better or who had lived a thousand years – mutant rats such as never existed and if all went well in the scheme of things never would.

He knew, intuitively and totally, the device was hopeless.

And, down the back of his neck, a giant blew a dying breath of terror. The chill of failure froze him as he sat rocking back and forth, on the floor of the motel room, listening to the far-off noise of the girl he had fallen in love with being sick.

TWENTY

Later, they had coffee. He and Lilo Topchev, Dr. Todt and the Red Army officer who was their warden and protector against the insanities within themselves, Red Army Intelligence Major Tibor Apostokagian Geschenko. The four of them drank what Lars Powderdry knew to be a toast to ruin.

Lilo said abruptly, 'It's a failure.'

'And how,' Lars nodded without meeting her gaze.

In a Slavic gesture, Geschenko patted the air, priest-like, with his open hand. 'Patience. By the way.' He nodded, and an aide approached their circular table with a homeopape – in Cyrillic type. Russian. 'An additional alien satellite is up,' Geschenko said. 'And it is reported that a field of some variety, a warpage of electromagnetic – I don't understand it, being no physicist. But it has affected your city New Orleans.'

'Affected how?'

Geschenko shrugged. 'Gone? Buried or hidden? Anyhow, communication is cut and sensitive measuring apparatus nearby records a lowering of mass. And an opaque barrier conceals what transpires, a field identified as connected with that of the satellites. Isn't this approximately what we foresaw?' He deliberately slurped his coffee.

'I don't understand,' Lars said tightly. And the drum of fear beat and beat inside him.

'Slavers.' Geschenko added, 'They are not *landing*. They are I think taking pieces of population, New Orleans first.' He shrugged. 'We will knock them down, don't worry. In 1941 when the Germans —'

'With a steam donkey-engine?' Lars turned to Lilo. 'This is the true, undefiled reason that moved you to try to kill me, isn't it? So we'd never have to arrive at this point, sit here and drink coffee like this!'

Major Geschenko said with psychological acumen, 'You give her an easy out, Mr. Lars. That is unhealthy, because she can divest herself further of responsibility.' To Lilo he said, 'That was *not* the reason.'

'Say it was,' Lars said to her.

'Why?'

'Because then I can think you wanted to spare us both even the *knowledge* of this. It was a form of mercy.'

'The unconscious,' Lilo said, 'has ways of its own.'

'No unconscious!' Major Geschenko said emphatically, reciting his doctrine. 'That's a myth. Conditioned response; you know that, Miss Topchev. Look, Mr. Lars; there's no merit in what you're trying to do. Miss Topchev is subject to the laws of the Soviet Union.'

Lars sighed, and from his pocket he brought out the rolled-up comic book which he had bought at the enormous news-counter at the space terminal. He passed it to Lilo: the Blue Cephalopod Man From Titan and His Astonishing Adventures Among the Fierce Protoplasms of Eight Deadly Moons. She accepted it curiously.

'What is it?' she asked him presently, large-eyed.

'A glimpse,' Lars said, 'into the outside world. What life would be like for you if you could come with me, leave this man and Peep-East.'

'*This* is what is for sale in Wes-bloc?'

'In West Africa, mostly,' he answered.

Lilo turned the pages, inspected the lurid and really downright dreadful drawings. Major Geschenko meanwhile stared off into space, lost in gloomy thought; his fine, clear face showed the despair which he had so far kept from his voice. He was, undoubtedly, thinking about the news from New Orleans ... as any sane man would. And the major was indubitably sane. He would not be looking at a comic book, Lars realized. But Lilo and I – we are not quite sane, at this point. And for good reason. Considering the magnitude of our spectacular failure.

He asked Lilo, 'You notice anything strange about that comic book?'

'Yes.' She nodded vigorously. 'They've used several of my sketches.'

'*Yours!*' He had noticed only his own weapons sketches. 'Let me look again.'

She showed him the page. 'See? My lobotomy gas.' She indicated Major Geschenko. 'They conducted tests on political prisoners and showed the results on TV. Just like this comic strip; it causes the victims to repeat endlessly the last series of instructions arising from the damaged cerebral cortex. The drawist has the Twin-brained Beasts From Io victims of this; he understood what weapon BBA-81D did, so he must have viewed the TV tape made in the Urals. But the tape was only shown last week.'

'Last week?' Incredulous, Lars took the comic book back. Obviously it had been printed longer ago than that. It carried last month's date, and sat on the newsstand for perhaps sixty days. All at once to Major Geschenko he said, 'Major, may I contact KACH?'

'Now? Immediately?'

'Yes,' Lars said.

Major Geschenko silently took the comic book from Lars and glanced through it. Then he rose and gestured; an aide stepped into existence and the two men discoursed in Russian.

'He's not asking for a KACH-man for you,' Lilo said then. 'He's telling the KVB to investigate this comic book firm, where it originates in Ghana.' She spoke to Major Geschenko in Russian herself. Lars felt, unhappily, the acute linguistic insularity of the American; Lilo was right. Mark of the province, he said to himself; and he wished to God he knew what they were saying. All three of them kept referring to the comic book and at last Major Geschenko handed it over to his aide.

The aide departed with it, rapidly. The door slammed shut, as if the aide were mad.

'That was mine,' Lars said. Not that it counted.

'A KACH-man will come,' Lilo said. 'But not immediately. Not what you asked for. They will conduct their own investigation and then let you make your try.'

Lars said to the powerful Red Army intelligence officer, 'I want to be returned to the jurisdiction of the FBI. Now. I insist on it.'

'Finish your coffee.'

'Something is wrong,' Lars said. 'Something about that comic book. I could tell by your manner; you discovered or thought something. What was it?' Turning to Lilo he said, 'Do you know?'

'They're upset,' Lilo said. 'They think KACH has been supplying repros to this comic-book firm. That irks them. They don't mind if Wes-bloc has access, but not this; this goes too far.'

'I agree,' Lars said. But I think there's more, he said to himself. I know there is; I saw too much agitation, here, just now.

'There is a time-factor,' Major Geschenko said, presently. He poured himself a fresh cup, but the coffee was utterly cold now.

'The comic-book firm got the sketches too soon?' Lars asked.

'Yes.' Major Geschenko nodded.

'Too soon even for KACH?'

'Yes.'

Stricken, Lilo said, 'I don't believe it.'

Major Geschenko glanced at her, briefly and without warmth.

'Not from them,' Lilo said. 'Surely we couldn't be.'

'The final episode in the magazine,' Major Geschenko said. 'The Blue Whatever-he-is-man devised as a temporary source of power, while imprisoned on a barren asteroid, a steam engine. To act as an agent by which to reactivate the dead transmitter of his half-demolished ship, the normal power supply having been rayed out of existence by the —' he grimaced – 'the Pseudonomic Flower-carnivores from Ganymede.'

Lars said, 'Then we are getting it from them. From the artist of that magazine.'

'Perhaps so,' Major Geschenko said, nodding very slowly, as if out of the most intense politeness he was willing to consider it – and for that reason only.

'Then no wonder —'

'No wonder,' Major Geschenko said, sipping cold coffee, 'that you can't perform your function. No wonder there is no weapon when we need it. *Must* have it. How could there be, from such a source?'

He raised his head, eyed Lars with a peculiarly bitter, accusing pride.

Lars said, 'But if we are simply reading some comic artist's mind, how could there be *anything*?'

'Oh, that artist,' Major Geschenko said disdainfully, 'he has much talent. An inventive mind. Don't ignore that. He's kept us going a long time, both of us, my friend. East *and* West.'

'This is the worst news —' Lars began.

'But interesting,' Major Geschenko said. He glanced from Lars to Lilo. 'Pitiful.'

'Yes, pitiful,' Lars said thickly.

TWENTY-ONE

After a pause Lilo said starkly, 'You realize what this means. Now they can go directly to him, whoever draws that ghastly, gutterish comic. They don't need us, Lars; not ever again.'

Major Geschenko murmured, with caustic but high-born politeness, 'Go to him for what, Miss Topchev? What do you think he has? Do you think he's held anything back?'

'There's no more,' Lars said. 'The man's in business, writing a comic strip. His inventions have been completely spurious all along.'

'But all along,' Major Geschenko pointed out in his urbane, mild, devastatingly insulting way, 'this was exactly proper for the need. Now that is no longer true. The Blue Cephalopod Man cannot fly through space and knock the alien satellites down with his fist. We are not able to call on him – he will not show up. A satire on ourselves has duped us for years. The artist will be amused. Obviously he is a degenerate. That vulgar strip – and I notice it is English-language, the official language of Wes-bloc – shows that.'

Lars said, 'Don't blame him if telepathically, in some crazy goddam way, we've been picking up his ideas.'

Lilo said, 'They won't "blame" him; they'll just shake him down. They'll pick him up and bring him to the Soviet Union, to the Pavlov Institute, try with all they have available to get out of him what they haven't got out of us. Just in case it *might* be there.' She added, '*I'm* glad I'm not him.' She seemed, in fact, relieved now. Because, as she understood the situation, the pressure was off her and to her, in her immaturity, that was what mattered.

'If you're so glad,' Lars said to her, 'at least don't show it. Try to keep it to yourself.'

'I'm beginning to think,' Lilo said, 'that it's exactly what they deserve.' She giggled. 'It's really funny. I'm sorry for that artist in Southern Ghana, but can't you laugh, Lars?'

'No.'

'Then you're as crazy as him.' She gestured in Major Geschenko's direction, contemptuously, with a new, spirited superiority.

'Can I make a vidphone call?' Lars asked Major Geschenko.

'I suppose.' Geschenko again beckoned to an aide, spoke to him in Russian; Lars found himself being escorted down a hallway to a public vidphone booth.

He dialed Lanferman Associates in San Francisco and asked for Pete Freid.

Pete looked overworked and not in the mood for receiving calls. Seeing who it was, he gave forth a meager gesture of salutation. 'What's she like?'

'She's young,' Lars said. 'Physically attractive, I would say sexy.'

'Then your problems are over.'

'No,' Lars said. 'Oddly, my problems aren't over. I have a job I want you to do. Bill me for it. If you can't do it yourself or won't do it —'

'Don't make a speech. Just say what it is.'

Lars said, 'I want every back issue of *The Blue Cephalopod Man from Titan* rounded up. A complete file from issue number one, volume one.' He added, 'It's a 3-D comic book. You know, the lurid kind that wiggles when you look at it. I mean, the girls wiggle – breasts, pelvic area, all there is to wiggle. The monsters salivate.'

'Okay.' Pete scratched himself a memo. '*The Blue Cephalopod Man from Titan*. I've seen it, although it's not made for North America. My kids seem to get hold of it anyhow. It's one of the worst, but it's not illegal, not outright pornographic. Like you say, the girls wiggle but at least they don't —'

'Go over every issue,' Lars said. 'With your best engineers. Thoroughly. List every weapons item employed in all the sequences. Check out which are ours and Peep-East's. Draw up accurate specs, anyhow as accurate as you can, based on the

131

data given in the comic book sequences.'

'Okay.' Pete nodded. 'Well, go ahead.'

'Make a third list of all weapons items that are *not* ours and are *not* Peep-East's. In other words unknown to us. Maybe there won't be any but maybe there will. Have them, if possible, made into accurate specs; I want mock-ups and—'

'Did you and Lilo come up with anything?'

'Yes.'

'Good.'

'It's called a steam engine. Donkey type.'

Pete regarded him. 'Seriously.'

'Seriously.'

'They'll massacre you.'

'I know that,' Lars said.

'Can you get away? Back to Wes-bloc?'

'I can try; I can run. But there's other things that are more important at this moment. Now listen. Job number two, which you will actually do first. Contact KACH.'

'Right.' Jot-jot.

'Have them investigate all persons responsible for preparing, drawing, making up the dummies, writing the script ideas. In other words, go into the human sources of all the material in the comic book *The Blue Cephalopod Man from Titan*.'

'Will do.' Pete scratched away.

'Urgently.'

'Urgently.' Pete wrote that. 'And report to whom?'

'If I'm back in Wes-bloc, to me. If not, then to you. Next job.'

'Shoot, Mr. God, sir.'

'Vidphone on an emergency line the S.F. branch of the FBI. Tell them to instruct their team here in the field at Fairfax, Iceland to —' And he stopped, because the screen had gone blank. The set was dead.

Somewhere along the line the Soviet secret police who had been monitoring the call had pulled the plug.

It was astonishing that they hadn't done so sooner.

He left the booth, stood pondering. Down the corridor waited two KVB men. No other way out.

Yet somewhere in Fairfax the FBI had holed itself up. If he somehow got to them he might be able to —

But they had orders to cooperate with the KVB. They would simply turn him back over to Major Geschenko.

It's still that wonderful world, he thought, in which everyone cooperates – unless you happen to be the sole person who has ceased to cooperate and who would like to get out. Because there is no longer an out; all the roads lead back here.

He might as well eliminate the middlemen and deal directly with Major Geschenko.

So, reluctantly, he returned to the motel room.

At the table Geschenko, Dr. Todt and Lilo Topchev still sat, drinking coffee and reading the homeopape. This time they were conversing in German. Multilingual bastards, Lars said to himself as he sat down.

'*Wie geht's?*' Dr. Todt asked him.

'*Traurig*,' Lilo said. '*Konnen Sie nicht sehen?* What happened, Lars? Did you phone up General Nitz and ask him to please take you home? And he said no, and don't bother me, because you're now under the jurisdiction of the KVB, even though Iceland is supposedly neutral ground. *Nicht wahr?*'

To Major Geschenko, Lars said, 'Major, I am officially asking permission to discuss my situation alone with a rep from the United States police agency, the FBI. Will you grant that?'

'Easily managed,' Geschenko said. A KVB man, abruptly entering the room, surprised all of them. Geschenko included. He approached the major, presenting him with typed, not a Xeroxed, document. 'Thank you,' Geschenko said, and silently read the document. Then he lifted his head to confront Lars. 'I think your idea is a good one – to sequester all the back-issues of *The Blue Cephalopod Man from Titan* and to have KACH run a thorough analysis on the strip's creators. We, of course, are already doing both ourselves, but there's no reason why your people can't duplicate it. However, to save time – and time, I should remind you, is in this case essential – I advance very respectfully the idea that you ask your business associates in San Francisco whom you just now conversed with to notify

133

us of any useable material which they might uncover. After all, it is an American city that has been the first object of attack.'

Lars said, 'If I can speak to an FBI man, yes. If not, no.'

'I told you already that it was easy to arrange.' Geschenko addressed his aide again in Russian.

Lilo said, 'He's telling him to go out, stay five minutes, return and say in English that the FBI entourage here at Fairfax can't be located.'

Glancing at her, Major Geschenko said irritably, 'In addition to all else you could be arraigned under Soviet law for interfering with security operations. It would be a charge of treason, punishable by death before a firing squad. So why don't you for once in your life shut up?' He looked genuinely angry; he had lost his poise and his face was dark red.

Lilo murmured. '*Sie konnen Sowjet Gericht und steck*' —'

Interrupting, Dr. Todt said firmly, 'My patient, Mr. Powderdry, seems under great stress, due especially to this last interchange. Would you object, Major, if I gave him a tranquilizer?'

'Go ahead, doctor,' Geschenko said grouchily. He waved curtly, dismissing his aide — without having reinstructed him, Lars observed.

From his black medical bag Dr. Todt brought several bottles, a flat tin, a number of folders of free samples the sort distributed by the large ethical pharmaceutical houses in incredible numbers all over the world, new drugs as yet untested and not on the market; he had, wearisomely, always been interested in the latest in medications. Mumbling, calculating to himself, Todt sorted among them, lost in his own idiosyncratic universe.

Again an aide brought Geschenko a document. He studied it silently, then said, 'I have preliminary information on the artist who is the creator of The Blue Man abomination. Would you care to hear it?'

'Yes,' Lars said.

'I couldn't care less,' Lilo said.

Dr. Todt continued to root about in his overfilled black medical bag.

Reading from the document presented him, Major Geschenko summarized for Lars' benefit the info which the Soviet intelligence-apparatus, acting at top speed, had assembled. 'The artist is named Oral Giacomini. A Caucasian of Italian origin who migrated to Ghana ten years ago. He is in and out of a mental institution in Calcutta – and not a reputable one at that. Without electroshock and thalamic-suppressors he would be in a complete autistic schizophrenic withdrawal.'

'Jeez,' Lars said.

'Further, he is an ex-inventor. For instance, his Evolution Rifle. He actually built one, about twelve years ago, had it patented in Italy. Probably for use against the Austro-Hungarian Empire.' Geschenko set down the document on the table; coffee stained it at once, but he did not seem to give a good goddam, Lars noticed; the major was as disgusted as he himself. 'Oral Giacomini's ideas, as analyzed by the second-rate psychiatrists at Calcutta, consist of worthless, grandiose, schizophrenic delusions of world-power. And this is the lunatic nonentity whose mentality you —' he shook his fist, futilely, at Lars and Lilo – 'have seen fit to tap as the inspiration for your "weapons"!'

'Well,' Lars said presently, 'that's the weapons fashion designing biz.'

Dr. Todt closed his medical bag at last and sat regarding them.

'You have my tranquilizer?' Lars asked. Dr. Todt had *something* in his hands, resting on his lap out of sight.

'I have here,' Dr. Todt said, 'a laser pistol.' He displayed it, pointing it at Major Geschenko. 'I knew I had it somewhere in my bag, but it was under everything else. You are under arrest, Major, for holding a Wes-bloc citizen captive against his will.'

From his lap he produced a second object, a minute audio communications-system, complete with microphone, earphone and antenna. Snapping it on he spoke into the flea-size mike. 'Mr. Conners? J. F. Conners, please?' He explained, for the benefit of Lars, Lilo and Major Geschenko, 'Conners is in charge of FBI operations here at Fairfax. Um. Mr. J. F. Conners? Yes. We are at the motel. Yes. Apt. six. Where they

135

first brought us. Evidently they plan to transport Mr. Powder-dry to the Soviet Union when they return Miss Topchev and are awaiting transport-connections at this moment. There are KVB agents all over so – well, okay. Thanks. Yes. And thank you again.' He shut off the communications-system and restored it to his medical bag.

They sat inertly, saying nothing, and then presently outside the door of the motel room there was a flurry of sharp, abrupt noise. Grunts, labored, muffled thumps, a voiceless cat-fight of confusion that lasted several minutes. Major Geschenko looked philosophical but not very happy. Lilo, on the other hand, seemed petrified; she sat bolt-upright, her face stark.

The door snapped spring-like open. An FBI man, one of those who had brought Lars to Iceland, peered in, laser pistol sweeping potentially everything in the room with its ability to include them all as targets. However, he did not fire but merely entered, followed by a second FBI man who had somehow, in what had happened, lost his tie.

Major Geschenko rose to his feet, unbuttoned his holster, silently turned over his side arm to the FBI men.

'We'll go back to New York now,' the first man said to Lars.

Major Geschenko shrugged. Marcus Aurelius could not have achieved more stoic resignation.

As Dr. Todt and Lars moved toward the door with the two FBI men, Lilo Topchev suddenly said, 'Lars! I want to come along.'

The two FBI men exchanged glances. Then one spoke into his lapel-mike, conversed inaudibly with an unseen superior. All at once he said brusquely to Lilo, 'They say okay.'

'You may not like it there,' Lars said. 'Remember, dear – we're both out of favor.'

'I still want to come,' Lilo said.

'Okay,' Lars said, and thought of Maren.

TWENTY-TWO

In the park in Festung, Washington, D.C. the aged, feeble, shabbily dressed war veteran sat mumbling to himself and watching the children playing, and then he saw, making their way without haste down the wide gravel path, two second lieutenants from the Wes-bloc Air Arm Academy, youths of nineteen with clean, scrubbed, beardless but arrestingly, unusually intelligent faces.

'Nice day,' the ancient hulk said to them, nodding.

They paused briefly. That was enough.

'I fought in the Big War,' the old man cackled, with pride. 'You never saw combat but I did; I was main-man for a frontline T.W.G. Ever seen a T.W.G. recoil 'cause of an overload, when the input-line circuit-breaker fails, and the induction field shorts? Fortunately I was off a distance so I survived. Field hospital. I mean a ship. Red Cross. I was laid up months.'

'Gee,' one of the shavetails said, out of deference.

'Was that in the Callisto revolt six years ago?' the other asked.

The ancient cobwebbed shape swayed with brittle mirth. 'It was sixty-three years ago. I been running a fixit shop since. Until I got to bleeding internally and had to quit except for small work. Apt appliances. I'm a first-rate swibble man; I can fix a swibble that otherwise —' He wheezed, unable to breathe momentarily.

'But sixty-three years ago!' the first shavetail said. He calculated. 'Heck, that was during World War Two; that was 1940.' They then both stared at the old veteran.

The hunched, dim, stick-like figure croaked, 'No, that was 2005. I remember because my medal says so.' Shakily, he groped at his tattered great-cloak. It seemed to disintegrate as he poked at it, turning further into dust. He showed them a small metal star pinned to his faded shirt.

Bending, the two young commissioned officers read the metal surface with its raised figures and letters.

'Hey, Ben. It does say 2005.'

'Yeah.' Both officers stared.

'But that's *next year*.'

'Let me tell you about how we beat 'em in the "Big War,"' the old vet wheezed, tickled to have an audience. 'It was a long war; sheoot, it seemed like it'd never end. But what can you do against T.G. warp? And that's what *they* found out. Were they surprised!' He giggled, wiped then at the saliva that had sputtered from his sunken lips. 'We finally came up with it; of course we had all those failures.' With disgust he hawked, spat onto the gravel. 'Those weapons designers didn't know a thing. Stupid bastards.'

'Who,' Ben said, 'was "the enemy"?'

It took a long time before the old veteran could grasp the nature of the question and when he did his disgust was so profound as to be overwhelming. He tottered to his feet, moved shufflingly away from the two young officers. '*Them*. The slavers from Sirius!'

After a pause the other second lieutenant seated himself on the other side of the old war veteran and then, thoughtfully, he said to Ben, 'I think —' He made a gesture.

'Yeah,' Ben said. To the old man he said, 'Pop. Listen. We're going below.'

'Below?' The old man cringed, confused and frightened.

'The *kremlin*,' Ben said. 'Subsurface. Where UN-W Natsec, the Board, is meeting. General Nitz. Do you know who General George Nitz is?'

Mumbling, the veteran pondered, tried to remember. 'Well, he was way up there,' he said finally.

'What year is this?' Ben said.

The old man eyed him gleefully. 'You can't fool me. This is 2068. Or —' The momentarily bright eyes dimmed over, hesitantly. 'No, it's 2067; you were trying to catch me. But you didn't, did you? Am I right? 2067?' He nudged the young

138

second lieutenant.

To his fellow officer, Ben said, 'I'll stay here with him. You get a mil-car, official. We don't want to lose him.'

'Right.' The officer rose, sprinted off in the direction of the *kremlin's* surface-installations. And the funny thing was he kept thinking over and over again, inanely, as if it had any bearing: What the hell was a swibble?

TWENTY-THREE

On the subsurface level of Lanferman Associates, more or less directly beneath the mid-California town of San Jose, Pete Freid sat at his extensive work-bench, his machines and tools inert, silent, off.

Before him lay the October 2003 copy of the uncivilized comic book, *The Blue Cephalopod Man from Titan*. At the moment, his lips moving, he examined the entertaining adventure, *The Blue Cephalopod Man Meets the Fiendish Dirt-Thing That Bored to the Surface of Io After Two Billion Years Asleep in the Depths!* He had reached the frame where the Blue Cephalopod Man, roused to consciousness by his side-kick's frantic telepathic efforts, had managed to convert the radiation-detecting portable G-system into a Cathode-Magnetic Ionizing Bi-polar Emanator.

With this Emanator, the Blue Cephalopod Man threatened the Fiendish Dirt-Thing as it attempted to carry off Miss Whitecotton, the mammate girlfriend of the Blue Man. It had succeeded in unfastening Miss Whitecotton's blouse so that one breast – and only one; that was International Law, the ruling applying severely to children's reading material – was exposed to the flickering light of Io's sky. It pulsed warmly,

139

wiggled as Pete squeezed the wiggling-trigger. And the nipple dilated like a tiny pink lightbulb, upraised in 3-D and winking on and off, on and off ... and would continue to do so until the five-year battery-plate contained within the back cover of the mag at last gave out.

Tinnily, in sequence, as Pete stroked the aud tab, the adversaries of the adventure spoke. He sighed. He had by now noted sixteen 'weapons' from the pages so far inspected. And meanwhile, New Orleans, then Provo, and now, according to what had just come over the TV, Boise, Idaho was missing. Had disappeared behind the gray curtain, as the 'casters and 'papes were calling it.

The gray curtain of death.

The vidphone on his desk pinged. He reached up, snapped it on. Lars' careworn face appeared on the screen.

'You're back?' Pete asked.

'Yes. In my New York office.'

'Good,' said Pete. 'Say, what line of work are you going to go into now that Mr. Lars, Incorporated of New York and Paris is kaput?'

'Does it matter?' Lars asked. 'In an hour I'm supposed to meet with the Board down below in the *kremlin*. They're staying perpetually subsurface, in case the aliens turn their whatever-it-is on the capital I'd advise you to stay underground, too; I hear the aliens' machinery doesn't penetrate subsurface.'

Pete nodded glumly. Like Lars, he felt somatically sick. 'How's Maren taking it?'

Lars, hesitating, said, 'I – haven't talked to Maren. The fact is, I brought Lilo Topchev back with me. She's here now.'

'Put her on.'

'Why?'

'So I can get a look at her, that's why.'

The sunny, uncomplicated face of a young girl, light-complexioned, with oddly astringent, watchful eyes and a tautly pursed mouth, appeared on the vidscreen. The girl looked scared and – tough. Wow, Pete thought. And you deliberately brought this kid back? Can you handle her? I doubt if I could, he decided. She looks difficult.

140

But that's right, Pete remembered. You like difficult women. It's part of your perverse make-up.

When Lars' features reappeared Pete said, 'Maren will disembowel you, you realize. No cover story is going to fool Maren, with or without that telepathic gadget she wears illegally.'

Lars said woodenly, 'I don't expect to fool Maren. But I frankly don't care. I really think, Pete, that these creatures, whatever they are and wherever they came from, these satellite-builders, have us.'

Pete was silent. He did not see fit to argue; he agreed.

Lars said, 'On the vidphone when I talked to Nitz he said something strange. Something about an old war veteran; I couldn't make it out. It had to do with a weapon, though; he asked me if I had ever heard of a device called a T.W.G. I said no. Have you?'

'No,' Pete said. 'There's absolutely no such thing, weapon-wise. KACH would have said.'

'Maybe not,' Lars said. 'So long.' He broke the connection at his end; the screen spluttered out.

TWENTY-FOUR

Security, Lars discovered when he landed, had been even further augmented; it took over an hour for him to obtain clearance. In the end it required personal, face-to-face recognition of who he was and what he had come for on the part of a long-time, trusted Board assistant. And then he was on his way down, descending to join what might well turn out to be, he realized, the final convocation of UN-W Natsec at its intact fullness.

The last decisions were now being made.

In the middle of his discourse General Nitz took a moment, unexpectedly, to single out Lars and speak to him directly. 'You missed a lot, due to your being away at Iceland. Not your fault. But something, as I indicated to you on the phone, has come up.' General Nitz nodded to a junior officer who at once snapped on an intrinsic, homeo-programmed, vidaud scanner with a thirty-inch screen, parked in one corner of the room, at the opposite corner from the instrument which linked the Board, when desired, with Marshal Paponovich and the SeRKeb in New Moscow.

The set warmed up.

An ancient man appeared on it. He was thin, wearing the patched remnants of some peculiar military uniform. Hesitantly he said, '... and then we clobbered them. They didn't expect that; they were having it easy.'

Bending, at General Nitz' signal, the junior officer stopped the Ampex aud-vid tape; the image froze, the sound ceased.

'I wanted you to get a look at him,' General Nitz said to Lars. 'Ricardo Hastings. Veteran of a war that took place sixty-some years ago ... in his view of it, at least. All this time, for months, years perhaps, this old man has been sitting every day on a bench in the public park just outside the surface installations of the citadel, trying to get someone to listen to him. Finally someone did. In time? Maybe. Maybe not. We'll see. It depends on what his brain, and our examination has already disclosed that he suffers from senile dementia, still contains by way of memory. Specifically, memory of the weapon which he serviced during the Big War.'

Lars said, 'The Time Warpage Generator.'

'There is little doubt,' General Nitz said, folding his arms and leaning back against the wall behind him, professor-wise, 'that it was through the action, perhaps accumulative and residual, of this weapon, of his constant proximity to it, especially to *defective* versions of it, that he wound up, in a way we don't understand, back here. In what, for him, is almost a century in the past. He is far too senile to notice; he simply does not understand. But that hardly matters. The "Big War" which for him took place years ago, when he was a young man, we have already established to be the war we are currently engaged in. Ricardo Hastings has already been able to tell us the nature and origin of our enemy; from him we've finally learned something, at long last, about the aliens.'

'And you hope,' Lars said, 'to obtain from him the weapon which got to them.'

'We hope,' Nitz said, 'for anything we can get.'

'Turn him over to Pete Freid,' Lars said.

General Nitz cupped his ear inquiringly.

'The hell with this talk,' Lars said. 'Get him to Lanferman Associates; get their engineers started working.'

'Suppose he dies.'

'Suppose he doesn't. How long do you think it takes a man like Pete Freid to turn a rough idea into specs from which a prototype can be made? He's a genius. He could take a child's drawing of a cat and tell you if the organism depicted covered its excretion or walked away and left it lying there. I have Pete Freid reading over back-issues of *The Blue Cephalopod Man from Titan*. Let's stop that and start him on Ricardo Hastings.'

Nitz said, 'I talked to Freid. I —'

'I know you did,' Lars said. 'But the hell with talk. Get Hastings to California or better yet get Pete here. You don't need me; *you don't need anyone in this room*. You need him. In fact I'm leaving.' He rose to his feet. 'I'm stepping out of this. So long, until you start Freid on this Hastings matter.' He at that point started, strode, toward the door.

'Perhaps,' General Nitz said, 'we will try you out on Hastings first. And then bring in Freid. While Freid is on his way here —'

'It takes only twenty minutes,' Lars said, 'or less to get a man from California to Festung, Washington, D.C.'

'But Lars. I'm sorry. The old man is senile. Do you literally, *actually*, know what that means? It appears to be almost impossible to establish a verbal bridge to him. So please, from the remains of his mind that are not accessible in the ordinary, normal —'

'Fine,' Lars said, deciding on the spot. 'But I want Freid

143

notified first. Now.' He pointed to the vidphone at Nitz' end of the table.

Nitz picked up the phone, gave the order, hung the phone up.

'One more thing,' Lars said. 'I'm not alone now.'

Nitz eyed him.

'I have Lilo Topchev with me,' Lars said.

'Will she work? Can she do her job here with us?'

'Why not? The talent's there. As much as there ever was in me.'

'All right.' Nitz decided. 'I'll have both of you taken into the hospital at Bethesda where the old man is. Pick her up. You can both go into that odd, beyond-my-comprehension trance-state. And meanwhile Freid is on his way.'

'Fine,' Lars said, satisfied.

Nitz managed to smile. 'For a prima donna you talk tough.'

'I talk tough,' Lars said, 'not because I'm a prima donna but because I'm too scared to wait. I'm too afraid they'll get us while we're *not* talking tough.'

TWENTY-FIVE

By government high-velocity hopper, piloted by a bored, heavy-set professional sergeant named Irving Blaufard, Lars raced back to New York and Mr. Lars, Incorporated.

'This dame,' Sergeant Blaufard said. 'Is she that Soviet weapons fashion designer? You know, *the* one?'

'Yes,' Lars said.

'And she 'coated?'

'Yep.'

'Wowie,' Sergeant Blaufard said, impressed.

The hopper, stone-like, dropped to the roof of the Mr. Lars, Incorporated building, the small structure among towering colossi. 'Sure a *little* place you got there, sir,' said Sergeant Blaufard. 'I mean, is the rest of it subsurface?'

'Afraid not,' Lars said stoically.

'Well, I guess you don't need no great lot of hardware.'

The hopper – expertly handled – landed on the familiar roof field. Lars jumped forth, sprinted to the constantly moving down-ramp, and a moment later was striding up the corridor toward his office.

As he started to open the office door Henry Morris appeared from the normally-locked side-exit. 'Maren's in the building.'

Lars stared at him, his hand on the doorknob.

'That's right,' Henry nodded. 'Somehow, maybe through KACH, she found out about Topchev coming back from Iceland with you. Maybe KVB agents in Paris tipped her off in vengeance. God only knows.'

'Has she got to Lilo yet?'

'No. We intercepted her in the outer public lobby.'

'Who's holding onto her?'

'Bill and Ed McEntyre, from the drafting department. But she's really sore. You wouldn't believe it was the same girl, Lars. Honest. She's unrecognizable.'

Lars opened his office door. At the far end, by the window, alone in the room, stood Lilo, gazing out at New York.

'You ready to go?' Lars said.

Lilo, without turning, said, 'I heard; I have terribly good hearing. Your mistress is here, isn't she? I knew this would happen. This is what I foresaw.'

The intercom on Lars' desk buzzed and his secretary Miss Grabhorn, this time with panic, not with disdain, said, 'Mr. Lars, Ed McEntyre says that Miss Faine got away from him and Bill Manfretti and she's out of the pub-lob and she's heading for your office.'

'Okay,' Lars said; he grabbed Lilo by the arm, propelled her out of the office and along the corridor to the nearest up-ramp. She came ragdoll-like, passively; he felt as if he were lugging a light-weight simulacrum devoid of live or motivation, a weirdly unpleasant feeling. Did Lilo not care any longer, or was this just too much for her? No time to explore the psychological ramifications of her inertness; he got her to the ramp and onto it and the two of them ascended, back up toward the roof with its field and waiting government hopper.

As he and Lilo emerged onto the roof, stepped from the up-ramp, a figure manifested itself at the up-terminus of the building's one alternate up-ramp, and it was Maren Faine.

As Henry Morris had said, she was difficult to recognize. She wore her high-fashion Venusian wubfur ankle-length cloak, high heels, a small hat with lace, large, hand-wrought earrings and, oddly, no make-up, not even lipstick. Her face had a lusterless, straw-like quality. A hint almost of the sepulcher, as if death had ridden with her across the Atlantic from Paris and then up here now to the roof; death perched in her eyes, gazing out fat-birdlike and impassive but with guileful determination.

'Hi,' Lars said.

'Hello, Lars,' Maren said, measuredly. 'Hello, Miss Top-chev.'

No one spoke for a moment. He could not recall ever having felt so uncomfortable in his entire life.

'What say, Maren?' he said.

Maren said, 'They called me direct from Bulganingrad. Someone at SeRKeb or acting for it. I didn't believe it until I checked with KACH.'

She smiled, and then she reached into her mailpouch-style purse which hung from her shoulder by its black leather strap.

The gun that Maren brought forth was positively the smallest that he had ever seen.

The first thought that entered his mind was that the damn thing was a toy, a gag; she had won it in a nickel gum machine. He stared at it, trying to make it out more exactly and remembering that he was after all a weapons expert, and then it came to him that it was genuine. Italian-made to fit into women's purses.

Beside him Lilo said, 'What is your name?' Her tone, addressed to Maren, was polite, rational, even kindly; it aston-

146

ished him and he turned to gape at her.

There was always something new to be learned about people. Lilo completely floored him; at this critical moment, as she and he faced Maren's tiny dangerous weapon, Lilo Topchev had become lady-like and mature, as socially graceful as if she had entered a party in which the most fashionable cogs abounded. She had risen to the occasion and it was, it seemed to him, a vindication of the quality, the essence, of the stuff of humanity itself. No one could ever again convince him that a human being was simply an animal that walked upright and carried a pocket handkerchief and could distinguish Thursday from Friday or whatever the criterion was ... even Ol' Orville's definition, cribbed from Shakespeare, was revealed for what it was, an insulting and cynical vacuity. What a feeling, Lars thought, not only to love this girl but also to admire her.

'I'm Maren Faine,' Maren said, matter-of-factly. *She* was not impressed.

Lilo hopefully extended her hand, evidently as a sign of friendship. 'I am very glad,' she began, 'and I think we can —'

Raising the tiny gun, Maren fired.

The filth-encrusted and yet clean-shiny little gadget expelled what once would have been certified as a dum-dum cartridge, in its primordial state of technological development.

But the cartridge had evolved over the years. It still possessed the essential ingredient – that of exploding when it contacted its target – but in addition it did more. Its fragments continued to detonate, reaping an endless harvest that spread out over the body of the victim and everything near him.

Lars dropped, fell away instinctually, turned his face and cringed; the animal in him huddled in a fetal posture, knees drawn up, head tucked down, arms wrapped about himself, knowing there was nothing he could do for Lilo. That was over, over forever. Centuries could pass like drops of water, unceasing, and Lilo Topchev would never reappear in the cycles and fortunes of man.

Lars was thinking to himself like some logical machine built

147

to compute and analyze coolly, despite the outside environment: I did not design this, not this weapon. This predates me. This is old, an ancient monster. This is all the inherited evil, carried here out from the past, carted to the doorstep of my life and deposited, flung to demolish everything I hold dear, need, desire to protect. All wiped out, just by the pressure of the first finger against a metal switch which is part of a mechanism so small that you could actually swallow it, devour it in an attempt to cancel out its existence in an act of oral greed – the greed by life for life.

But nothing would cancel it now.

He shut his eyes and remained where he was, not caring if Maren chose to fire again, this time at him. If he felt anything at all it was a desire, a yearning that Maren would shoot him.

He opened his eyes.

No longer the up-ramp. The roof field. No Maren Faine, no tiny Italian weapon. Nothing in its ravaged state lay nearby him; he did not see the remnants, sticky organic, lashing and decomposed and newly-made, the bestial malignancy of the weapon's action. He saw, but did not understand, a city street, and not even that of New York. He sensed a change in temperature, in the composition of the atmosphere. Mountains ice-topped, remote, were involved; he felt cold and he shivered, looked around, heard the honking racket of surface traffic.

His legs, his feet ached. And he was thirsty.

Ahead, by an autonomic drugstore he saw a public vidphone booth. Entering it, his body stiff, creaking with fatigue and soreness, he picked up the directory, read its cover.

Seattle, Washington.

And time, he thought. How long ago was that? An hour? Months? Years; he hoped it was as long as possible, a fugue that had gone on interminably and he was now old, old and rotted away, wind-blown, discarded. This escape should not have ever ended, not even now. And in his mind the voice of Dr. Todt came incredibly, by way of the parapsychological power given him, that voice as it had on the flight back from Iceland hummed and murmured to itself: words not understandable to him, and yet their terrible tone, their world, as

148

Dr. Todt had hummed to himself an old ballad of defeat. *Und die Hunde schnurren an den alten Mann.* And then all at once Dr. Todt in English told him. *And the dogs snarl*, Dr. Todt said, within his mind. *At the aged man.*

Dripping a coin into the phone-slot he dialed Lanferman Associated in San Francisco.

'Let me talk to Pete Freid.'

'Mr. Freid,' the switchboard chick at Lanferman said brightly, 'is away on business. He cannot be reached, Mr. Lars.'

'Can I talk to Jack Lanferman, then?'

'Mr. Lanferman is also – I guess I can tell you, Mr. Lars. Both of them are at Festung, Washington, D.C. They left yesterday. Possibly you could contact them there.'

'Okay,' he said. 'Thanks. I know how.' He rang off.

He next called General Nitz. Step by step his call mounted the ladder of the hierarchy, and then, when he was about ready to call it quits and hang up, he found himself facing the C. in C.

'KACH couldn't find you,' Nitz said. 'Neither could the FBI or the CIA.'

'The dogs snarled,' Lars said. 'At me. I heard them. In all my life, Nitz, I never heard them before.'

'Where are you?'

'Seattle.'

'Why?'

'I dunno.'

'Lars, you really look awful. And do you know what you're doing or saying? What's this about "dogs"?'

'I don't know what they are,' he said. 'But I did hear them.'

General Nitz said, 'She lived six hours. But of course there was never any hope and anyhow now it's over; or maybe you know this.'

'I don't know anything.'

'They held up the funeral services thinking you might show up, and we kept on trying to locate you. Of course you realize what happened to you.'

'I went into a trance-state.'

'And you're just now out?'

Lars nodded.

'Lilo is with —'

'What?' Lars said.

'Lilo is at Bethesda. With Ricardo Hastings. Trying to develop a useable sketch; she's produced several so far but —'

Lars said, 'Lilo is dead. Maren killed her with an Italian Beretta pelfrag .12 pistol. I saw it. I watched it happen.'

Regarding him intently, General Nitz said, 'Maren Faine fired the Beretta .12 pelfrag pistol that she carried with her. We have the weapon, the fragments of the slug, her fingerprints on the gun. But she killed herself, not Lilo.'

After a pause Lars said, 'I didn't know.'

'Well,' General Nitz said, 'when that Beretta went off, somebody had to die. That's how those pelfrag pistols are. It's a miracle it didn't get all three of you.'

'It was suicide! Deliberate. I'm sure of it.' Lars nodded. 'She probably never intended to kill Lilo, even if she thought so herself.' He let out a ragged sigh of weariness and resignation. The kind of resignation that was not philosophical, not stoical, but simply a giving up.

There was nothing to be done. During his trance-state, his fugue, it had all happened. Long, long ago. Maren was dead; Lilo was at Bethesda; he, after a timeless journey to nowhere, into emptiness, had wound up in down-town Seattle, as far away, evidently, as he could manage to get from New York and what had taken place – or what he had imagined had taken place.

'Can you get back here?' General Nitz said. 'To help out Lilo? Because it's just not coming; she takes her drug, that East German goofball preparation, goes into her trance, placed of course in proximity to Ricardo Hastings with no other minds nearby to distract her. And yet when she sobers up she has only —'

'The same old sketches. Derived from Oral Giacomini.'

'No.'

'You're sure?' His limp, abused mind came awake.

'These sketches are entirely different from anything she's

150

done before. We've had Pete Freid examine them and he agrees. And she agrees. And they're always the same.'

He felt horror. 'Always what?'

'Calm down. Not of a weapon at all, not of anything remotely resembling a "Time Warpage Generator." They're of the physiological, anatomical, organic substance of —' General Nitz hesitated, trying to decide whether to say it over the probably-KVB-tapped vidphone.

'Say it,' Lars grated.

'Of an android. An unusual type, but still an android. Much like those that Lanferman Associates uses subsurface in its weapons proving. You know what I mean. As human as possible.'

Lars said, 'I'll be there as soon as I can.'

TWENTY-SIX

At the immense parking-field atop the military hospital he was met by three snappily uniformed young Marines. They escorted him, as if he were a dignitary, or perhaps, he reflected, a criminal, or a gestalt of both combined, down-ramp at once to the high security floor on which *it* was taking place.

It. No such word as *they*. Lars noted the attempt to dehumanize the activity which he had come here to involve himself in.

He remarked to his escort of Marines, 'It's still better than falling into the hands, if they do have hands, of alien slavers from some distant star system.'

'What is, sir?'

'Anything,' Lars said.

The tallest Marine, and he really was tall, said, 'You've got

151

something there, sir.'

As their group passed through the final security barrier, Lars said to the tall Marine. 'Have you seen this old war vet, this Ricardo Hastings, yourself?'

'For a moment.'

'How old would you guess he is?'

'Maybe ninety. Hundred. Older, even.'

Lars said, 'I've never seen him.'

Ahead, the last door – and it had some super-sense, in that it anticipated exactly how many persons were to be allowed through – swung temporarily open; he saw white-clad medical people beyond. 'But I'll make a bet with you,' he said, as the sentient door clicked in awareness of his passage through. 'As to Ricardo Hastings' age.'

'Okay, sir.'

Lars said, 'Six months.'

The three Marines stared at him.

'No,' Lars said. 'I'll revise that. Four months.'

He continued on, then, leaving his escort behind, because ahead he saw Lilo Topchev.

'Hi,' he said.

At once she turned. 'Hi.' She smiled, fleetingly.

'I thought you were at Piglet's house,' he said. 'Visiting Piglet.'

'No,' she said. 'I'm at Pooh's house visiting Pooh.'

'When that Beretta went off —'

'Oh Christ I thought it was me, and you thought it was me; you were sure and you couldn't look. Should it have been me? Anyhow it wasn't. And I would have done the same; I wouldn't have looked if I thought it was headed at you. What I've decided, and I've been thinking and thinking, never stopping thinking ... I've been just so damn worried about you, where you went – you had your trance and you simply wandered off. But thinking about her I decided she must never have fired that pelfrag pistol before. She must not have had any idea what it did.'

'And now what?'

'I've been working. Oh God how I've been working. Come

152

on into the next room and meet him.' She somberly led the way. 'Did they tell you I haven't had any luck?'

Lars said, 'It could be worse, considering what's being done to us every hour or so.' On the trip east he had learned the extent of the population-volume now converted out of existence – as far as Earth was concerned – by the enemy. It was grotesque. As a calamity it had no historic parallel.

'Ricardo Hastings says they're from Sirius,' Lilo said. 'And they are slavers, as we suspected. They're chitinous and they have a physiological hierarchy dating back millions of years. On the planets of their system, a little under nine light-years from here, warm-blooded life forms never evolved past the lemur stage. Arboreal, with fox-muzzles, most types nocturnal, some with prehensile tails. So they don't regard us as anything but sentient freaks. Just highly-organized work-horse organisms that are somewhat clever manually. They admire our *thumb*. We can do all sorts of essential jobs; they think of us the way we do rats.'

'But we test rats all the time. We try to learn.'

'But,' Lilo said, 'we have lemur curiosity. Make a funny noise and we pop our heads out of our burrows to see. They don't. It seems that among the chitinous forms, even highly evolved, you're still dealing primarily with reflex-machines. Talk to Hastings about it.'

Lars said, 'I'm not interested in talking to him.'

Ahead, beyond an open door, sat – a stick-like clothed skeleton, whose dim, retracted, withered-pumpkin, caved-in face revolved slowly as if motor-driven. The eyes did not blink. The features were unstirred by emotions. The organism had deteriorated into a mere perceiving-machine. Sense-organs that swiveled back and forth ceaselessly, taking in data although how much eventually reached the brain, was recorded and understood, God knew. Perhaps absolutely none.

A familiar personality manifested itself, clipboard in hand. 'I knew you'd eventually reappear,' Dr. Todt said to Lars, but nevertheless he looked drastically relieved. 'Did you walk?'

'Must have,' Lars said.

'You don't remember.'

153

Lars said, 'Nothing. But I'm tired.'

'There's a tendency,' Dr. Todt said, 'for even major psychoses to get walked off, given enough time. The Nomadic Solution. It's just that there's not enough time in most cases. As for you, there's no time at all.' He turned then to Ricardo Hastings. 'As to him, what are you going to try first?'

Lars studied the huddled old figure. 'A biopsy.'

'I don't understand.'

'I want a tissue-sample taken. I don't care what from, any part of him.'

'Why?'

Lars said, 'In addition to a microscopic analysis I want it carbon-dated. How accurate is the new carbon-17-B dating method?'

'Down to fractions of a year. Months.'

'That's what I thought. Okay, there won't be any sketches, trances, any other activity from me, until the carbon dating results are in.'

Dr. Todt gestured. 'Who can question the ways of the Immortals?'

'How long will it take?'

'We can have the results by three this afternoon.'

'Good,' Lars said. 'I'll go get a shower, a new pair of shoes and I think a new cloak. To cheer myself up.'

'The shops are closed. People are warned to stay underground during the emergency. The areas taken now include —'

'Don't rattle off a list. I heard on the trip here.'

'Are you honestly not going to go into a trance?' Dr. Todt said.

'No. There's no need to. Lilo's tried it.'

Lilo said, 'Do you want to see my sketches, Lars?'

'I'll look at them.' He held out his hand and after a moment a pile of sketches was given to him. He leafed briefly through them and saw what he had expected – no less, no more. He set them down on a nearby table.

'They *are* of an elaborate construct,' Dr. Todt pointed out.

'Of an android,' Lilo said hopefully, her eyes fixed on Lars.

154

He said, 'They're of him.' He pointed at the ancient huddled shape with its ceaselessly revolving, turret-like head. 'Or rather it. You didn't pick up the contents of its mind. You picked up the anatomical ingredients constituting its biochemical basis. What makes it go. The artificial mechanism that it is.' He added. 'I'm aware that it's an android, and I know the carbon-dating of the biopsy sample will bear this out. What I want to learn is its exact age.'

After a time Dr. Todt said hoarsely, 'Why?'

'How long,' Lars said, 'have the aliens been in our midst?'

'A week.'

'I doubt,' Lars said, 'whether an android as perfectly built as this one could be thrown together in a week.'

Lilo said presently, 'Then the builder knew – if you're right —'

'Oh, hell,' Lars said. 'I'm right. Look at your own sketches and tell me if they aren't of "Ricardo Hastings." I mean it. Go ahead.' He picked up the sketches, presented them to her; she accepted them reflexively and in a numbed, sightless way turned from one to the next, nodding faintly.

'Who could have built such a successful android?' Dr. Todt said, glancing over Lilo's shoulder. 'Who has the facilities and the capabilities, not to mention the – inspirational talent?'

Lars said, 'Lanferman Associates.'

'Anyone else?' Dr. Todt said.

'Not that I know of.' Through KACH, he of course had a fairly accurate concept of Peep-East's facilities. They had nothing comparable. *Nothing* was comparable to Lanferman Associates, which after all stretched subsurface from San Francisco to Los Angeles: an economic, industrial organism five hundred miles long.

And making androids which could pass, under close scrutiny, as authentic human beings, was one of their major enterprises.

All at once Ricardo Hastings croaked. 'If it hadn't been for that accident when that power-surge overloaded the —'

Lars, walking over, interrupted him, abruptly. 'Are you operating on intrinsic?'

155

The ancient, dim eyes confronted him. But there was no answer; the sunken mouth did not stir, now.

'Come on,' Lars said. 'Which is it, intrinsic or remote? Are you homeostatic or are you a receptor for instructions coming from an outside point? Frankly, I'd guess you're fully intrinsic. Programmed in advance.' To Lilo and Dr. Todt he said, 'That explains what you call its "senility." The repetition of certain stereotyped semantic units over and over again.'

Ricardo Hastings mumbled wetly, 'Boy, how we clobbered them. They didn't expect it; thought we were washed up. Our weapons fashion designers, they hadn't come through. The aliens thought they could just walk right in and take over, but we showed them. Too bad you people don't remember; it was before your time.' He – or it – chuckled, sightlessly staring at the floor, its mouth twitching in a grimace of delight.

'I don't,' Lars said, pausing, 'buy the idea of the time-travel weapon anyhow.'

'We got the whole mess of them,' Ricardo Hastings mumbled. 'We warped their goddam satellites entirely out of this time-vector, a billion years into the future, and they're still there. Heh-heh.' His eyes, momentarily, lit with a spark of life. 'Orbiting a planet that's uninhabited except by maybe spiders and protozoa. Too bad for them. We caught their ships of the line, too; with the T.W.G. we sent *them* into the remote past; they're set to invade Earth around the time of the trilobite. They can win that easy. Beat the trilobites, club them into submission.' Triumphantly, the old veteran snorted.

At two-thirty, after a wait which Lars would not have undergone again at any price, the carbon-dating of the tissue taken from the old man's body was brought in by a hospital attendant.

'What does it show?' Lilo asked, standing up stiffly, her eyes fixed on his face, trying to apprehend his reaction, to share it with him.

Lars handed her the single sheet. 'Read it yourself.'

Faintly she said, 'You tell me.'

'The microscopic analysis showed it to be indubitably human, not syntho – that is, android – tissue. The carbon-17-B

156

dating procedures, applied to the tissue-sample, indicate that the sample is one hundred and ten years to one hundred and fifteen years old. And possibly – but not probably – even older.'

Lilo said, 'You were wrong.'

Nodding, Lars said, 'Yes.'

To himself, Ricardo Hastings chuckled.

TWENTY-SEVEN

On this score, Lars Powderdry said to himself, I have failed as completely as, formerly, I let them down authentic, in time of need weapons-wise. There has never been one point at which I have really served them, except of course in the old situation, the benign game which Peep-East and Wes-bloc played all those years, the Era of Plowsharing in which we duped the multitude, the pursaps everywhere, for their own good, at the expense of their own proclivities.

I did bring Lilo to Washington, though, he thought. Maybe that should be entered in the record-books as an achievement. But – what has that accomplished, besides the hideous suicide of Maren Faine, who had every reason for living on, enjoying a full and happy life?

To Dr. Todt, Lars said, 'My Escalatium and my Conjorozine, please. Twice the customary dose.' To Lilo he said, 'And that East German firm's product that you have a monopoly on. I want you to double your intake of it at this time. It's the only way I can think of to increase our sensitivity and I want us to be as sensitive as our systems can withstand. Because we'll probably only make one real try.'

'I'll agree to that,' Lilo said somberly.

The door shut after Todt and the hospital staff-members. He and Lilo, with Ricardo Hastings, were sealed off.

'This may,' he said to Lilo, 'kill either or both of us, or impair us permanently. Liver-toxicity or brain —'

'Shut up!' Lilo said. And, with a cup of water, downed her tablets.

He did the same.

They sat facing each other for a moment, ignoring the mumbling, slavering old man between them.

'Will you ever recover,' Lilo asked presently, 'from her death?'

'No. Never.'

'You blame me? No, you blame yourself.'

'I blame her,' Lars said. 'For owning that miserable, lousy little Beretta in the first place; no one should carry a weapon like that or even own it; we're not living in a jungle.'

He ceased. The medication was taking effect; it paralyzed like an enormous overdose of phenothiazine, his jaws and he shut his eyes, suffering. The dose, much too much, was carrying him off and he could no longer see, experience the presence of, Lilo Topchev. Too bad, he thought. And it was regret, and pain, that he experienced, rather than fear, as the cloud condensed around him, the familiar descent – or was it ascent? – now heightened, magnified out of all reasonable proportion, by the deliberate over-supply of the two drugs.

I hope, he hoped, that she isn't going to be required to endure this, too; I hope it is easier on her – knowing that would make it easier on me.

'We really blasted them,' Ricardo Hastings mumbled, chuckling, wheezing, dribbling.

'Did we?' Lars managed to say.

'Yes, Mr. Lars,' Ricardo Hastings said. And the garrulous, trivial mumble, somehow, seemed cleared, became lucid. 'But not with any so-called "Time Warpage Generator". That is a fabrication – in the bad sense. I mean a cover-story.' The old man chuckled, but this time harshly. Differently.

Lars, with extreme difficulty, said, 'Who are you?'

'I am an ambulatory toy,' the old man answered.

158

'*Toy!*'

'Yes, Mr. Lars. Originally an ingredient of a war-game invented by Klug Enterprises. Sketch me, Mr. Lars. Your compatriot, Miss Topchev, is no doubt sketching, but merely repeating, without realizing it, the worthless visual-presentation formerly produced ... and ignored by everyone but you. She is drawing *me*. You were absolutely right.'

'But you're old.'

'A simple technical solution presented itself to Mr. Klug. He foresaw the possibility – in fact the inevitability – of an application of the new dating-test by carbon-17-B. So my constituents are modifications of organic matter slightly in excess of one hundred years vintage. If that expression doesn't disgust you.'

'It doesn't disgust me,' Lars said, or thought. He could no longer tell if he were actually speaking aloud. 'I just plain don't believe it,' he said.

'Then,' Hastings said, 'consider this possibility. I am an android, as you suspected, *but built over a century ago.*'

'In 1898?' Lars asked with bottomless scorn. 'By a buggy-whip concern in Nebraska?' He laughed, or tried to, anyhow. 'Give me another one. Another theory that fits what you know and I know to be the facts.'

'This time would you like to try the truth, Mr. Lars? Hear it openly, with nothing held back? Do you feel capable? Honestly? You're *sure*?'

After a pause Lars said, 'Yes.'

The soft, whispering voice, perhaps composed of nothing more in this deep-trance relationship than a thought, informed him, 'Mr. Lars, I am Vincent Klug.'

TWENTY-EIGHT

'The small-time operator. The marginal, null-credit, kicked-around toy man himself,' Lars said.

'That's right. Not an android but a man like yourself, only old, very old. At the end of my days. Not as you've met me and seen me subsurface, at Lanferman Associates.' The voice was weary, toneless. 'I have lived a long time and seen a good deal. I saw the Big War, as I said. As I told everyone and anyone who would listen to me as I sat on the park bench. I knew eventually the proper person would come along, and he did. They got me inside.'

'And you were main-man in the war?'

'No. Not for that or any weapon. A time-warpage instrument exists – will exist – but it will not factor in the Big War against the Sirius slavers. That part I made up. Sixty-four years from now, in 2068, I will make use of it to return.

'You don't understand. I can come back here from 2068; I've done so. Here I am. But I can't bring anything. Weapon, artifact, news, idea, the most minuscule technological pursap entertainment novelty – *anything*.' The voice was savage, roused to bitterness. 'Go ahead! Telepathically pry at me, tinker with my memory and knowledge of the next six decades. Obtain the specs for the Time Warpage Generator. And take it to Pete Freid at Lanferman Associates in California; get a rush-order on it, have a prototype made right up and used on the aliens. Go ahead! You know what'll happen? It will cancel me out, Mr. Lars.' The voice cut at him, deafening him, cruel. Corrupted by vindictiveness and the futility of the situation. 'And when it cancels me out, by instigating an alternate time-path, it will cancel the weapon out, too. And an oscillation, *with me caught in it*, will be erected in perpetuity.'

Lars was silent. He did not dispute; it seemed evident and

he accepted it.

'Time-travel,' said the ancient, decayed Klug of sixty-four years from now, 'is one of the most rigidly limited mechanisms arrived at by the institutional research system. Do you want to know exactly *how* limited I am, Mr. Lars, at this moment in time, which is for me over sixty years in the past? *I can see ahead and I can't tell anything* – I can't inform you; I can't be an oracle. Nothing! All I can do, and this is very little, but it may be enough – I know, as a matter of fact, whether it'll be enough, but I can't even risk telling you this – is call your attention to some object, artifact or aspect of your present environment. You see? It must *already* exist. Its presence must not in any way be dependent on my return here from your future.'

'Hmm,' Lars said.

' "Hmm." ' Vincent Klug sneered, mocking him.

'Well,' Lars said, 'What can I say? It's been said; you just now went through it, stage by stage.'

'Ask me something.'

'Why?'

'Just ask! I came back for a reason; isn't that obvious? God, I'm tied in knots by this damn principle – it's called —' Klug broke off, choked with impotence and fury.

'I can't even give you the name of the principle that limits me,' he said, with descending strength. The battle to communicate – but not to communicate beyond the narrow, proper line – was palpably draining him rapidly.

Lars said, 'Guessing games. That's right; you like games.'

'Exactly.' A resurgence of energy pulsed in the dry, dust-like voice. 'You guess. I either answer or I don't.'

'Something exists now, in our times, in 2004.'

'Yes!' Frenzied, vibrant, humming excitement; the furious regathering of the life-force in response.

'You, in this time period, are not a cog. You're on the outside and that is a fact. You've tried to bring it to UN-W Natsec's attention but since you're not a cog, no one will listen.'

'*Yes!*'

'A working prototype?'

'Yes. By Pete Freid. On his own time. After Jack Lanferman gave him permission to use the company shops. He's so goddam good; he can build so goddam fast.'

'Where is the device now?'

A long silence. Then, haltingly, in agony, 'I – am – afraid to – say too much.'

'Pete has it.'

'N-no.'

'Okay,' Lars pondered. 'Why didn't you try to communicate with Lilo?' he asked. 'When she went into a trance-state and probed at your mind?'

'Because,' Klug whispered wearily in his dry, rushing voice, 'she is from Peep-East.'

'But the Prototype —'

'I see ahead. This weapon, Mr. Lars, is for Wes-bloc alone.'

'Is the weapon,' Lars said, 'in Festung, Washington, D.C. at this time?'

Witheringly, the voice of the ancient Vincent Klug eaten away by the destroyer retorted, 'If it were I would not be talking to you. I would have returned to my own period.' He added, 'Frankly, I have plenty to lose by being here, my friend. The medical science of my own era is capable of sustaining my life on an endurable basis. That, however, is not the case in this year, 2004.' His voice pulsated with the rhythm of fatigue and contempt intertwined.

'Okay, this device,' Lars said – and sighed – 'this weapon originates from my own time and not from the future. You've had the prototype made. Presumably it works. So you've either taken it back to your own tiny factory or wherever it is you operate!' For a long time he considered, recapitulating in his mind over and over again. 'All right,' he said. 'I don't need to ask you any more; we don't need to strain it. Better not to take any more chances. You agree?'

'I agree,' Klug said, '*if* you feel you can continue on your own – with what you now know *and no more*.'

'I'll find it.'

Obviously he had to immediately approach the Vincent

Klug of this period, drag the device out of him. But – and he saw it already – the Vincent Klug of 2004, having invented the device, would not recognize it as a weapon.

He would not therefore know which object was wanted; Klug might, in his typical, zany, marginal operations, possess a dozen, two dozen, constructs in every possible stage all the way from the rough sketch, the drafting board, to the final autofac-run retail-sales production items themselves.

He had broken contact with the ancient Vincent Klug of 2068 prematurely.

'Klug,' he said instantly, urgently. 'What kind of toy is it? A hint! Give me some clue. A board game? A war game?' His listened.

In his ears, as spoken words, not telepathically received thoughts, the cracked, senile voice mumbled, 'Yeah, we really clobbered them, those slavers; they sure didn't expect us to come up with anything.' The old man wheezing, chuckling with delight. 'Our weapons fashions designers. What a wash-out they were. Or so the aliens thought.'

Lars shaking, opened his eyes. His head ached violently. In the glare of the overhead light he squinted in pain. He saw Lilo Topchev beside him, slouched inert, her fingers holding a pen ... against a blank, untouched piece of white paper.

The trance-state, telepathic rapport with the obscured, inner mind of the old 'war veteran' Vincent Klug, had ended.

Looking down, Lars saw his own hand as it gripped a pen, his own sheet of paper. There was no sketch, of course; he was not surprised by that.

But the paper was not blank.

On it was a scrawled, labored sentence, as if the awkward, unskilled fingers of a child had gripped the pen, not his.

The sentence read:

> *The* (unreadable,
> a short word) *in*
> *the maze.*

The *something* in the maze, he thought. Rat? Possibly. He seemed to make out an *r*. And the word consisted of three letters, the second of which – he was positive, now, as he scrutinized it – was *a*.

Unsteadily, he rose, made his way from the room; he opened door after door, at last found someone, a hospital orderly.

'I want a vidphone,' Lars said.

He sat, finally, at a table on which rested an extension phone. With shaking fingers he dialed Henry Morris at his New York office.

Presently he had Henry on the screen.

'Get hold of that toy-maker Vincent Klug,' Lars said. 'He has a kids' product, a maze of some kind. It's gone through Lanferman Associates and come out. A working model exists. Pete Freid made it.'

'Okay,' Henry said, nodding.

'In that toy,' Lars said, 'there's a weapon. One we can use against the aliens – and win. Don't tell Klug why you want it. When you have it, mail it to me at Festung, Washington, D.C. by 'stant mail – so there's no time-lapse.'

'Okay,' Henry Morris said.

After he had rung off, Lars sat back, once more picked up the sheet of paper, re-examined his scrawled sentence. What in God's name was that blurred word? Almost he had it . . .

'How do you feel?' Lilo Topchev appeared, bleary-eyed, rubbing her forehead, smoothing back her rumpled hair. 'God, I'm sick. And again I got nothing.' She plopped herself down opposite him, rested her head in her hands. Then, sighing, she roused herself, peered to see the paper he held. 'You derived this? During the trance-state?'

She frowned, her lips moving. '*The* – something – *in the maze*. That second word.' For a time she was silent, and then she said, 'Oh. I see what it says.'

'You do?' He lowered the sheet of paper, and for some reason felt cold.

'The second word is *man*,' Lilo said. '*The man in the maze*; that's what you wrote during the trance. I wonder what it means.'

TWENTY-NINE

Later, subsurface, Lars sat in one of the great, silent meeting-chambers of the inner citadel, the *kremlin* of Fortress Washington, D.C., the capital city of all Wes-bloc with its two billion. (Less than that now, a substantial portion. But as to this Lars averted his thoughts; he kept his attention elsewhere.)

He sat with the unwrapped 'stant mail parcel from Henry Morris before him. A note from Henry informed him that this object was the sole maze-toy produced by Klug Enterprises and made up by Lanferman Associates in the last six years.

This small, square item was it.

The printed brochure from Vincent Klug's factory was included. Lars had read it several times.

The maze was simply enough in itself, but it represented for its trapped inhabitant an impenetrable barrier. Because the maze was inevitably one jump ahead of its victim. The inhabitant could not win, no matter how fast or how cleverly or how inexhaustibly he scampered, twisted, retreated, tried again, sought the one right (didn't there have to be a one right?) combination. He could never escape. He could never find freedom. Because the maze, ten-year-battery powered, constantly shifted.

Some toy, Lars thought. Some idea of what constitutes 'fun.'

But this was nothing; this did not explain what he had here on the table before him. For this was a psychologically sophisticated toy, as the brochure put it. The novelty angle, the inspired ingredient by which the toy-maker Vincent Klug expected to pilot this item into a sales success, was the empathic factor.

Pete Freid, seated beside Lars, said, 'Hell, I put it together.

165

And I don't see anything about it that would make it a weapon of war. And neither did Vince Klug, because I discussed it with him, before I made this prototype and after. I know darn well he never intended that.'

'You're absolutely correct,' Lars said. Because why at this period in his life-track should the toy-maker Vinvent Klug have any interest in weapons of war? But the later Vincent Klug —

He knew better.

'What kind of a person is Klug?' Lars asked Pete.

Pete gestured. 'Hell, you've seen him. Looks like if you stuck a pin in him he'd pop and all the air would come out.'

'I don't mean his physical looks,' Lars said. 'I mean what's he like inside? Down deep, the machinery that makes him run.'

'Strange, you putting it like that.'

'Why?' Lars felt sudden uneasiness.

'Well, it reminds me of one of the projects he brought to me long time ago. Years ago. Something he was eternally puttering around with but finally gave up. Which I was glad of.'

'Androids,' Lars said.

'How'd you know?'

'What was he going to do with the androids?'

Pete scratched his head, scowling. 'I could never quite figure it out. But I didn't like it. I told him no, every time.'

'You mean,' Lars said, 'he wanted you to build them? He wanted Lanferman Associates to utilize its expertise in that line, on his android project, but for some strange reason he never —'

'He was vague. Anyhow he wanted them really human-like. And I always had that uneasy feeling about it.' Pete was still scowling. 'Okay, I admit there's layers and layers to Klug. I've worked with him but I don't pretend to understand him, any more than I ever figured out what he had in mind with his android project. Anyhow, he did abandon it and turned to —' he gestured toward the maze – 'this.'

Well, Lars thought, so that explains Lilo's android sketches.

General Nitz, who had been sitting silently across from

them, said, 'The person who operates this maze – if I understand this right, he assumes an emotional identity with that thing.' He pointed at the tiny inhabitant, now inert because the switch was off. 'That creature, there. What is that creature?' He peered intently, revealing for the first time to Lars that he was slightly nearsighted. 'Looks like a bear. Or a Venusian wub; you know, those roly-poly animals that the kids love ... there's a phenotypal enclave of them here at the Washington zoo. God, the kids never get tired of watching that colony of wubs.'

Lars said, 'That's because the Venusian wub possesses a limited telepathic faculty.'

'That's so,' General Nitz agreed. 'As does the Terran porpoise, as they finally found out; it's not unique. Incidentally, that was why people kept feeling the porpoise was intelligent. Without knowing why. It was —'

Lars moved the switch to on, and in the maze the roly-poly wub-like, bear-like, furry, loveable creature began to move. 'Look at it go,' Lars said, half to himself.

Pete chuckled as the roly-poly creature bounced rubberballwise from a barrier which unexpectedly interceded itself in its path.

'Funny,' Lars said.

'What's the matter?' Pete asked him, puzzled at his tone, realizing that something was wrong.

Lars said, 'Hell, it's amusing. Look at it struggle to get out. Now look at this.' Studying the brochure, he ran his hands along both sides of the frame of the maze until he located the studs. 'The control on the left increases the difficulty of the maze. And the perplexity, therefore, of its victim. The control on the right decreases —'

'I *made* it,' Pete pointed out. 'I know that.'

'Lars,' General Nitz said, 'you're a sensitive man. That's why we call you "difficult." And that's what made you a weapons fashion medium.'

'A prima donna,' Lars said. He did not take his eyes from the wub-like, bear-like, roly-poly victim within the altering barriers that constituted the utterly defeating configuration of the maze.

Lars said, 'Pete. Isn't there a telepathic element built into this toy? With the effect of hooking the operator?'

'Yeah, to a certain extent. It's a low-output circuit. All it creates is a mild sense of identification between the child who's operating the maze with the creature trapped.' To General Nitz he explained, 'See, the psychiatric theory is that this toy teaches the child to care about other living organisms. It fosters the empathic tendencies inherent in him; he wants to help the creature, and that stud on the right permits him to do so.'

'However,' Lars said, 'there is the other stud. On the left.'

'Well,' Pete said condescendingly, 'that's technically necessary because if you just had a decrease-factor the creature would get right out. The game would be over.'

'So toward the end,' Lars said, 'to keep the game going, you stop pressing the decrease stud and activate the increase, and the maze-circuitry responds by stepping up the difficulty which the trapped creature faces. So, instead of fostering sympathetic tendencies in the child, it could foster sadistic tendencies.'

'No!' Pete said instantly.

'Why not?' Lars said.

'Because of the telepathic empathy-circuit. Don't you get it, you nut? The kid running the maze *identifies* with the victim. He's it. It's him in the maze; that's what empathy means – you know that. Hell, the kid would no more make it tough for that little critter than he'd – stab himself.'

'I wonder,' Lars said, 'what would happen if the telepathic empathy-circuit's output were stepped up.'

Pete said, 'The kid would be hooked deeper. The distinction, on an emotional level, between himself and the victim there in that maze —' He paused, licked his lip.

'And suppose,' Lars continued, 'the controls were also altered, so that both studs tended, but in a diffuse manner, only to augment the difficulty which the maze-victim is experiencing. Could that be done, technically-speaking?'

After a while Pete said, 'Sure.'

168

'And run off autofac-wise? In high-production quantity?'
'Why not?'

Lars said, 'This roly-poly Venusian wub creature. It's non-Terran, an organism alien to us. And yet because of the telepathic faculty it possesses it creates an empathic relationship with us. Would such a circuit, as represented here in this toy, tend to affect *any* highly-evolved sentient life form the same way?'

'It's possible.' Pete nodded. 'Why not? Any life form that was intelligent enough to receive the emanations would be affected.'

'Even a chitinous semi-reflex machine life form?' Lars said. 'Evolved from exoskeleton pregenitors? Not mammals? Not warm-blooded?'

Pete stared at General Nitz. 'He wants to step up the output,' he said excitedly, stammering in anger, 'and rewire the manual controls so that the operator is hooked deep enough not to break away when he wants to, and can't ease the severity of the barriers inhibiting the goddam maze-victim – and the result —'

'It could induce,' Lars said, 'a rapid, thorough mental disintegration.'

'And you want Lanferman Associates to reconstruct this thing and run it off in quantity on our autofac system. And distribute it to them.' Pete jerked his thumb upward. 'Okay. But we can't distribute it to the aliens from Sirius or whatever they are; that's beyond our control.'

General Nitz said, 'But *we* can. There is one way. Quantities of these can be available in population centers that the aliens acquire. So when they get us they get these, too.'

'Yeah,' Pete agreed.

General Nitz said to him, 'Get on it! Get building.'

Glumly, Pete stared at the floor, his jaw working. 'It's reaching them where they have a decent streak. This —' he gestured furiously at the maze-toy on the table – 'wouldn't work on them otherwise. Whoever dreamed this up *is getting at living creatures through their good side*. And that's what I don't like.'

Reading the brochure which had accompanied the maze-toy General Nitz said, ' "This toy is psychologically sophisticated in that it teaches the child to love and respect, to cherish, other living creatures, not for what they can do for him, but for themselves." ' He folded up the brochure, tossed it back to Lars, asked Pete, 'by when?'

'Twelve, thirteen days.'

'Make it eight.'

'Okay. Eight.' Pete reflected, licked his parched lower lip, swallowed and said, 'It's like booby-trapping a crucifix.'

'Cheers,' Lars said. And, manipulating the two studs, one on either side of the maze, he confronted the appealing, roly-poly wub-like victim with a declining difficulty. He made it easier and easier until it seemed the victim was about to reach the exit.

And then, at that moment, Lars touched the stud on the left. The circuitry of the maze inaudibly shifted – and a last and totally unexpected barrier dropped in the victim's path, halting him just as he perceived freedom.

Lars, the operator, linked by the weak telepathic signal emanating from the toy, felt the suffering – not acutely, but enough to make him wish he had not touched the left-handed stud. Too late now, though; the victim of the maze was once again openly entangled.

No doubt about it, Lars realized. This does, as the brochure says, teach sympathy and kindness.

But now, he thought, it is *our* turn to work on it. We cogs, we who are the rulers of this society; we who hold literally in our hands the responsibility of protecting our race. Four billion human beings who are looking to us. And – we do not manufacture toys.

THIRTY

After the alien slavers from Sirius had withdrawn their satellites – at the end there had been eight satellites orbiting the sky of earth – the life of Lars Powderdry began to sink back into normalcy.

He felt glad.

But very tired, he realized one morning as he woke slowly up in his bed in his New York apartment, and saw beside him the tumble of dark hair which was Lilo Topchev's. Although he was pleased – he liked her, loved her, was happy in a life commingled with hers – he remembered Maren.

And then he was not so pleased.

Sliding from bed he walked from the bedroom and into the kitchen. He poured himself a cup of the perpetually hot and fresh coffee maintained by one small plowshared gadget wired onto the otherwise ordinary stove.

Seated at the table, alone, he drank the coffee and gazed out the window at the high-rise conapt buildings to the north.

It would be interesting, he mused, to know what Maren would have said about our weapon in the Big War, the way in which we caused them to lay off. We made ourselves *un*valuable. Presumably the chitinous citizens of Sirius' planets are still slavers, still posting satellites in other peoples' skies.

But not here.

And UN-W Natsec, plus the cogs of Peep-East in all *their* finery, were still considering the utility of introducing The Weapon into the Sirius system itself . . .

I think, he thought, Maren would have been amused.

Sleepily, blinking in perplexity, Lilo, in her pink nightgown, appeared at the kitchen door. 'No coffee for me?'

'Sure,' he said, rising to get a cup and saucer for her. 'Do you know what the English word "to care" comes from?' he said, as he poured her coffee for her from the obedient gadget wired to the stove.

'No.' She seated herself at the table, looked gravely at the ashtray with its moribund remains of discarded, yesterday's cigars and winced.

'The Latin word *caritas*. Which means love or esteem.'

'Well.'

'St. Jerome,' he said, 'used it as a translation of the Greek word *agape* which means even more.'

Lilo drank her coffee, silently.

'*Agape*,' Lars said, standing at the window and looking out at the conapts of New York, 'means reverence for life; something on that order. There's no English word. But we still possess the quality.'

'Hmm.'

'And,' he said, 'so did the aliens. And that was the handle by which we grabbed and destroyed them.'

'Fix an egg.'

'Okay.' He punched buttons on the stove.

'Can an egg,' Lilo said pausing in her coffee-drinking, 'think?'

'No.'

'Can it feel what you said? *Agape*?'

'Of course not.'

'Then,' Lilo said, as she accepted the warm, steaming, sunny-side-up egg from the stove, plate included, 'if we're invaded by sentient eggs we'll lose.'

'Damn you,' he said.

'But you love me. I mean, you don't mind; in the sense that I can be what I am and you don't approve but you let me anyhow. Bacon?'

He punched more buttons, for her bacon and for his own toast, applesauce, tomato juice, jam, hot cereal.

'So,' Lilo decided, as the stove gave forth its steady procession of food as instructed, 'you don't feel *agape* for me. If, like you said, *agape* means *caritas* and *caritas* means to care. You wouldn't care, for instance, if I —' She considered. 'Suppose,' she said, 'I decided to go back to Peep-East, instead of run-

172

ning your Paris branch, as you want me to. As you keep urging me to.' She added, thoughtfully, 'So I'd even more fully replace her.'

'That's not why I want you to head the Paris branch.'

'Well ...' She ate, drank, pondered at length. 'Perhaps not, but just now, when I came in here, you were looking out the window and thinking. What if she was still alive. Right?'

He nodded.

'I hope to God,' Lilo said, 'that you don't blame me for her doing that.'

'I don't blame you,' he said, his mouth full of hot cereal. 'I just don't understand where the past goes when it goes. What happened to Maren Faine? I don't mean what happened that day on the up-ramp when she killed herself with that —' he eradicated a few words which came, savagely, to mind – 'that Beretta. I mean. Where is she? Where's she gone?'

'You're not completely awake this morning. Did you wash your face with cold water?'

'I did everything that I'm going to do. I just don't understand it; one day there was a Maren Faine and then there wasn't. And I was in Seattle, walking along. I never saw it happen.'

Lilo said, 'Part of you saw it. But even if you didn't see it, the fact remains that now there is no Maren Faine.'

He put down his cereal spoon. 'What do I care? I love you! And I thank God – I find it incredible – that it wasn't you who were killed by that pelfrag cartridge, as I first thought.'

'If she had lived, could you have had us both?'

'Sure!'

'No. Impossible. How?'

Lars said, 'I would have worked it somehow.'

'Her by day, me at night? Or her on Mondays, Wednesdays, Fridays, me on —'

'The human mind,' he said, 'couldn't possibly be defeated by that situation, if it had the chance. A reasonable chance, without that Beretta and what it did. You know something that old Vincent Klug showed me, when he came back as that old war veteran, so-called, that Ricardo Hastings? It's impossible to go back.' He nodded.

'But not yet,' Lilo said. 'Fifty years from now, maybe.'

'I don't care,' he said. 'I just want to see her.'

'And then what?' Lilo asked.

'Then I'd return to my own time.'

'And you're going to idle away your life, for fifty years or however long it is, waiting for them to invent that Time Warpage Generator.'

'I've had KACH look into it. Somebody's undoubtedly already doing basic research on it. Now that they know it exists. It won't be long.'

'Why,' Lilo said, 'don't you join her?'

At that he glanced up, startled. 'I am not kidding,' Lilo said. 'Don't wait fifty years —'

'More like forty, I calculate.'

'That's too long. Good God, you'll be over seventy years old!'

'Okay,' he admitted.

'My drug,' Lilo said quietly. 'You remember; it's lethal to your brain metabolism or some damn thing – anyhow three tablets of it and your vagus nerve would cease and you'd die.'

After a pause he said, 'That's very true.'

'I'm not trying to be cruel. Or vengeful. But – I think it would be smarter, saner, the better choice, to do that, take three tablets of Formophane than to wait forty to fifty years, drag out a life that means absolutely nothing —'

'Let me think it over. Give me a couple of days.'

'You see,' Lilo said, 'not only would you be joining her immediately, without waiting more years than you've lived already, but – you'd be solving your problems the way she solved hers. So you'd have that bond with her, too.' She smiled, grimly. Hatingly.

'I'll give you three tablets of Formophane right now,' she said, and disappeared into the other room.

He sat at the kitchen table, staring down at his bowl of cooling cereal and then all at once she was back. Holding out something to him.

He reached up, took the tablets from her, dropped them into

174

the shirt-pocket of his pajamas.

'Good,' Lilo said. 'So that's decided. Now I can go get dressed and ready for the day. I think I'll talk to the Soviet Embassy. What's that man's name? Kerensky?'

'Kaminsky. He's top-dog at the embassy.'

'I'll inquire through him if they'll take me back. They have some idiots they're using in Bulganingrad as mediums, but they're no good – according to KACH.'

She paused. 'But of course it's not the same as it was. It'll never be like that again.'

THIRTY-ONE

He held the three tablets of Formophane in his hand and considered the tall, cool glass of tomato juice on the table before him. He tried to suppose – as if one really could – how it would be, swallowing the tablets here and now, as she – the girl in the bedroom, whatever her name was – dressed for the day ahead.

While she dressed, he died. That simple. That simple, anyhow, to the easy scene-fabrication faculty available within the psychopathically-glib human mind.

Lilo paused at the bedroom door, wearing a gray wool skirt and slip, barefoot. She said, 'If you do it I won't grieve and hang around forty years waiting for that Time Warpage Generator so I can go back to when you were alive. I want you to be certain of that, Lars, before you do it.'

'Okay.' He hadn't expected her to. So it made no difference.

Lilo, remaining there at the door, watching him, said, 'Or maybe I will.'

Her tone, it seemed to him, was not contrived. She was

175

genuinely considering it, how she would feel, what it would be like. 'I don't know. I guess it would depend on whether Peep-East takes me back. And if so, what my life there would be like. If it was like the way they treated me before —' She pondered. 'I couldn't stand that and I'd begin to remember how it was here with you. So maybe I would; yes, I think I would start grieving for you, the way you are for her.' She looked up at him, alertly. 'Consider this aspect before you take those Formophane tablets.'

He nodded in agreement; it had to be considered.

'I really have been happy here,' Lilo said. 'It's been nothing like life was at Bulganingrad. That awful "classy" apartment I had – you never saw it, but it was ugly. Peep-East is a tasteless world.'

She came padding out of the bedroom toward him. 'I tell you what. I've changed my mind. If you still want me to I will take charge of the Paris office.'

'Meaning what?'

'Meaning,' Lilo said levelly, 'that I will do exactly what I said I wouldn't do. I'll replace her. Not for your sake but for mine, so I don't wind up in an apartment in Bulganingrad again.' She hesitated and then said, 'So I don't wind up the way you are, sitting there in your pajamas with those tablets in your hand, trying to decide whether you want to wait out the forty years or take care of it right now. You see?'

'I see.'

'Self-preservation.'

'Yes.' He nodded.

'I have that instinct. Don't you? Where is it in you?'

He said, 'Gone.'

'Gone even if I head the Paris branch?'

Reaching for the glass of tomato juice with one hand he put the three tablets in his mouth with the other, lifted the glass ... he shut his eyes, felt the cool, wet rim of the glass against his lips and thought then of the hard, cool can of beer that Lilo Topchev had so long ago presented him that first moment together in Fairfax when they met. When, he thought, she tried to kill me.

'Wait,' Lilo said.

He opened his eyes, holding in the three tablets, undissolved because they were hard-coated for easier swallowing, on his tongue.

'I have,' Lilo said, 'a gadget plowshared from item – well, it doesn't matter much which. You've used it before. In fact I found it here in the apartment. Ol' Orville.'

'Sure,' he said, mumbling because of the tablets. 'I know, I remember Ol' Orville. How is Ol' Orville, these days?'

Lilo said, 'Ask his advice before you do it.'

That seemed reasonable. So carefully he spat out the undissolved tablets and restored them, stickily, to his pajama pocket, sat waiting while Lilo went and got the intricate electronic quondam guidance-system, now turned household amusement and crypto-deity, Ol' Orville. The featureless little head that, and Lilo did not know this, he had last consulted in company with Maren Faine.

She set Ol' Orville before him on the breakfast table.

'Ol' Orville,' Lars said, 'how in hell are you today?' You who were once weapon-design-sketch number 202, he thought. First called to my attention, in fact, by Maren. You and your fourteen-thousand – or is it sixteen or eighteen? – minned parts, you poor plowshared freak. Castrated, like me, by the system.

'I am fine,' Ol' Orville replied telepathically.

'Are you the same, the very same Ol' Orville,' Lars said, 'that Maren Faine —'

'The same, Mr. Lars.'

'Are you going to quote Richard Wagner in the original German again to me?' Lars said. 'Because if you are, this time it won't be enough.'

'That is right,' Ol' Orville's thoughts croaked in his brain. 'I recognize that. Mr. Lars, do you care to ask me a distinct question?'

'You understand the situation that faces me?'

'Yes.'

Lars said, 'Tell me what to do.'

There was a long pause as the enormous number of superlatively miniaturized components of the original guidance-system of item 202 clacked away. He waited.

'Do you want,' Ol' Orville asked him presently, 'the elaborated, fully documented answer with all the citations included, the original source-material in Attic Greek, Middle-Low-High German and Latin of the —'

'No,' Lars said. 'Boil it down.'

'One sentence?'

'Or less. If possible.'

Ol' Orville answered, 'Take this girl, Lilo Topchev, into the bedroom and have sexual intercourse with her.'

'Instead of —'

'Instead of poisoning yourself,' Ol' Orville said. 'And also instead of wasting forty years waiting on something which you had already decided to abandon – *and you have ignored this, Mr. Lars* – when you went to Fairfax to see Miss Topchev the first time. You had *already* stopped loving Maren Faine.'

There was silence.

'Is that true, Lars?' Lilo asked.

He nodded.

Lilo said, 'Ol' Orville is smart.'

'Yes,' he agreed. He rose to his feet, pushed his chair back, walked toward her.

'You're going to follow its advice?' Lilo said. 'But I'm already half-dressed; we have to be at work in forty-five minutes. Both of us. There isn't time.'

She laughed happily, however, with immense relief.

'Oh yes,' Lars said. And picked her up in his arms, lugged her toward the bedroom. 'There's just barely enough time.' As he kicked the bedroom door shut after them he said, 'And just barely enough is enough.'

THIRTY-TWO

Far below Earth's surface in drab, low-rent conapt 2A in the least-desirable building of the wide ring of substandard housing surrounding Festung, Washington, D.C., Surley G. Febbs stood at one end of a rickety table at which sat five didascalic individuals.

Five motley, assorted persons, plus himself. But they had, however, been certified by Univox-50R, the official government computer, as able to represent the authentic, total trend of Wes-bloc buying-habits.

This secret meeting of these six new concomodies was so illegal as to beggar description.

Rapping on the table, Febbs said shrilly, 'The meeting will now come to order.'

He glanced up and down in a severe fashion, showing them who was in charge. It was he, after all, who had brought them, in the most circumspect manner possible, with every security precaution that a genuine uniquely clever human mind (his) could devise, together in this one dingy room.

Everyone was attentive – but nervous, because God knew the FBI or the CIA or KACH might burst in the door any moment despite the inspired security precautions of their leader, Surley G. Febbs.

'As you know,' Febbs said, his arms folded, feet planted wide apart so as to convincingly demonstrate that he was solidly planted here, was not about to be swept away by the hired creeps of any institutional police force, 'it is illegal for we six concomodies even to know one another's names. Hence, we shall begin this confabulation by reciting our names.' He pointed to the woman seated closest to him.

Squeakily, she said, 'Martha Raines.'

Febbs pointed to the next person in turn.

'Jason Gill.'

'Harry Markison.'

'Doreen Stapleton.'

'Ed. L. Jones.' The last man, at the far end, spoke firmly. And that was that. In defiance of the law of Wes-bloc and its police agencies they knew one another by name.

Ironically, since the Emergency had passed, the UN-W Natsec Board now 'allowed' them to enter the *kremlin* and officially participate in its meetings. And that's because individually, Febbs realized as he looked around the rickety table, each of us possesses nothing. *Is* nothing. And the Board knows it. But all six of us together —

Aloud he said commandingly, 'Okay; let's begin. Every one of you when you walked through this door brought your component of that new weapon, that item 401 they call the Molecular Restriction-Beam Phase-Inverter. Right? I saw a paper bag or neutral, ordinary-looking plastic carton under everyone's arm. Correct?'

Each of the five concomodies facing him mumbled a *yes, Mr. Febbs* or nodded or both. In fact each had placed his package on the table, in plain sight, as a show of courage.

Febbs instructed in a sharp, emotion-laden voice, 'Open them up. Let's see the contents!'

With shaking fingers and great trepidation, the paper bags and cartons were opened.

On the table rested the six components. When assembled (assuming that someone in this room could accomplish this) they formed the dread new Molecular Restriction-Beam Phase-Inverter.

Tapes of the tearwep in action at Lanferman Associates' huge subsurface proving-levels indicated that no defense against it existed. And the entire UN-W Natsec Board, including the six at-last-allowed-in concomodies, had solemnly viewed those tapes.

'Our task,' Febbs declared, 'of rebuilding these components back to form the original tearwep falls naturally onto myself. I personally shall take full responsibility. As you all know, the next formal meeting of the Board is one week from today. So

180

we have less than seven days in which to reassemble the Molecular Restriction-Beam Phase-Inverter, item 401.'

Jason Gill piped, 'You want us to stick around while you put it back together, Mr. Febbs?'

'You may if you so desire,' Febbs said.

Ed Jones said, 'Can we offer suggestions? The reason I ask that is, see, my job in real life – I mean before I was a concomody – was standby electrician at G.E. in Detroit. So I know a little about electronics.'

'You may offer suggestions,' Febbs decided, after some thought. 'I will permit it. But you understand our sacred pact. As a political organization we are to allow policy to be decided by our elected leader without bureaucratic hampering type restrictions. Correct?'

Everyone mumbled *correct*.

Febbs was that unhampered, unbureaucratically restricted, elected leader. Of their clandestine political revolutionary-type organization which (after long debate) had titled itself, menacingly, the BOCFDUTCRBASEBFIN, The Benefactors of Constitutional Freedoms Denied Under the Contemporary Rule By a Small Elite By Force If Necessary. Cell One.

Picking up his component and Ed Jones', Febbs seated himself and reached into the bin of brand-new tools which at great cost the organization had provided itself. He brought out a long, slender, tapered, German-made screwdriver with autonomic clockwise or anti-clockwise rotational action (depending on which way you pressed the plastic handle) and began his work.

Reverently, the other five members of the organization watched.

An hour later Surley G. Febbs grunted sweatily, wiping his forehead with his handkerchief as he halted to take a breather, said, 'This will take time. It isn't easy. But we're getting there.'

Martha Raines said nervously, 'I hope a roving, random police monitor doesn't happen to cruise by above-surface and pick up our thoughts.'

Politely, Jones pointed and said, 'Um, I believe that doodad

181

there fits up against that template. See where those screw-holes are?'

'Conceivably so,' Febbs said. 'This brings me to something I intended to take up later. But since I'm pausing for a while I might as well say it to you all now.' He glanced around at them to be sure he had their individual, undivided attention, and then spoke as authoritatively as possible. Given a man of his ability and knowledge this was very authoritative. 'I want all of you comprising Cell One clear in your minds as to the exact type of socio-economic, pol-struc of society we shall install in place of the undemo-tyr by the privileged cog elite which now holds power.'

'You tell 'em Febbs,' Jones said encouragingly.

'Yeah,' Jason Gill agreed. 'Let's hear once again! I like this part, what happens *after* we run 'em out of office with this item 401.'

With superlative calm, Febbs continued, 'Everyone on the UN-W Natsec Board will of course be tried as war criminals. We've agreed on that.'

'Yeah!'

'It is Article A in our Constitution. But as to the rest of the cogs, especially those Commie bastards in Peep-East that traitor General Nitz is so pally with. Like that Marshal Paponovich or whatever his name is. Well, like I've explained to you in our past secret meetings down here —'

'Right, Febbs!'

'— they're really going to get it. They're the worst. But mainly we have to seize — and I demand absolute obedience on this, because this is tactically crucial — we initially must gain control of the ENTIRE SUBSURFACE INSTALLATIONS OF LANFERMAN ASSOCIATES IN CALIFORNIA, because as we all know, it's from there the new weapons come. Like this 401 they stupidly turned over to us for — ha-ha — "plowsharing." I mean, we don't want them to build any *more* of these.'

Martha Raines asked timidly, 'And what do we do after we, ah, seize Lanferman Associates?'

Febbs said, 'Thereupon we then arrest their hired stooge,

182

that Lars Powderdry. And then we compel him to start designing weapons for *us*.'

Harry Markison, a middle-aged businessman with a certain amount of commonsense, spoke up. 'But the weapon by which we won what they are now calling "The Big war" with —'

'Get to it, Markison.'

'It, uh, wasn't designed by Mr. Lars, Incorporated. Originally it was some sort of maze invented by some non-cog toy-manufacturing outfit, Klug Enterprises. So – don't we have to beware that this Klug fella —'

'Listen,' Febbs said quietly. 'I'll tell you the real scoop on that. But now I'm busy.'

He then picked up a small Swedish watchmaker's screwdriver and resumed the task of reassembling weapon 401. He ignored the other five concomodies. There was no more time for blabbing; work had to be done, if their blitz-swift coup against the cog elite was to be successful. And it would be.

Three hours later, with most of the components (in fact all except one fast, outlandish, goose-neck-squash-like geegaw) assembled ready for all systems go, with Febbs wet with perspiration and the other five concomodies out of their minds or bored or restless, depending on their natures, there sounded – shockingly, making the room suddenly deathly still – a knock at the door.

Laconically, Febbs grunted, 'I'll handle this.' From the tool bin he lifted a beautifully balanced Swiss chrome-steel hammer and walked slowly across the room, past the rigid, pale, other five concomodies. He unbolted, unfastened, untied the triple-locked door, opened it a crack, peered out into the gloomy hall.

A spic-and-span-new shiny autonomic 'stant mail delivery robot stood there, waiting.

'Yes?' Febbs inquired.

The 'stant mail robot whirred, 'Parcel for Mr. Surley Grant Febbs. Registered. Sign here if you are Mr. Febbs or if not Mr. Febbs then on line two instead.' It presented a form, pen and flat surface of itself on which to scribble.

Zap   183

Laying down the hammer Febbs said, turning briefly to the other five concomodies, 'It's okay. More tools we ordered, probably.' He signed the form, and the autonomic 'stant mail delivery robot handed him a brown-paper-wrapped package.

Febbs shut the door, stood shakily holding the package, then shrugged in courageous defiance. He walked unconcernedly back to where he had been sitting.

'You've got guts, Febbs,' Ed Jones declared, expressing the sentiments of the group. 'I was sure it was an *Einsatzgruppe* from KACH.'

'In my opinion,' Harry Markison said, with overwhelming relief, 'it looked to be the goddam *Soviet* secret police, the KVB. I've got a brother-in-law in Estonia —'

Febbs said, 'They're just not smart enough to pinpoint our meetings. History will deal them out, evolution-wise to make way for superior forms.'

'Yeah,' Jones agreed. 'Like look how long it took them to come up with a weapon to defeat the alien slavers from Sirius with.'

'Open the package,' Markison said.

'In time,' Febbs said. He fitted the squash-like geegaw in place and mopped his drenched, steaming forehead.

'When do we act, Febbs?' Gill asked. They all sat eyes fixed on Febbs, waiting for his decision. Aware of this, he felt relaxed. The pressure was off.

'I've been thinking,' Febbs said, in his most Febbs-ish manner. It had been deep thinking, indeed. Reaching out, he picked up the weapon, tearwep item 401, held it cradled, his hand on the trigger.

'I required the five of you,' he said, 'because I had to obtain all six components that constitute this weapon. However —'

Pressing the trigger he demolecularized, by means of the wide-angle setting of the phase-inversion beam emanating from the muzzle of the weapon, his fellow five concomodies at their seats here and there around the rickety table.

It happened soundlessly. Instantly. As he had anticipated. The vid and aud tapes from Lanferman Associates, shown to

184

the Board, had indicated these useful aspects of item 401's action.

There was now left only Surley G. Febbs. And armed with Earth's most modern, fashionable, advanced, soundless, instant weapon. Against which no defense was yet known ... even to Lars Powderdry, whose business it was to conjure up such things.

And you, Mr. Lars, Febbs said to himself, *are next*.

He laid the weapon down carefully and, with calm hands, lit another cigarette. He regretted that there was no longer anyone in the room to witness his rational, precise movements – anyone but himself, anyhow.

And then, because obviously now he had time to spare, Febbs reached out, picked up the brown-paper-wrapped package which the autonomic 'stant mail delivery robot had brought and set it directly before him. He unwrapped it, slowly, leisurely, meditating in his infinitely subtle mind on the future which lay so close ahead.

He was frankly puzzled by what he found within the wrappings. It was not additional tools. It was nothing he, or the now nonexistent organization FUCFDUTCRBASEBFIN, Cell One, had ordered.

It was in fact a toy.

Specifically, he discovered as he lifted the lid of the brightly colored, amusing box, it was a product of the marginal toy-maker, Klug Enterprises. A game of some kind.

A child's maze.

He felt, immediately, on an instinctive level – because after all he was no ordinary man – acute, accurate, intuitive dismay. But not sufficiently acute, accurate or intuitive enough to cause him to hurl the box aside. The impulse was there. But he did not act on it – because he was curious.

Already he had seen that this was no common maze. It intrigued his uniquely subtle, agile mind. It held him gripped so that he continued to peer at the maze, then at the instructions on the inside lid of the box.

'You are the world's foremost concomody,' a telepathic voice sounded in his mind, emanating from the maze itself.

185

'You are Surley Grant Febbs. Right?'

'Right,' said Febbs.

'It is you,' the telepathic voice continued, 'who make the primary decision as to the worthwhileness of each consumer commodity newly introduced on the market. Right?'

Febbs, feeling a cold bite of caution over his heart, nevertheless nodded. 'Yes, that's so. They have to come to me first. That's my job on the Board – I'm the current concomody A. So they give me the important components.'

The telepathic voice said, 'Vincent Klug of Klug Enterprises, a small firm, would therefore, Mr. Febbs, like you to examine this new game, The Man In The Maze. Please determine whether in your expert opinion it is ready for marketing. A form is provided on which you may transcribe your reactions.'

Febbs said haltingly, 'You mean you want me to *play* with this?'

'That is exactly what we want. Please press the red button on the right side of the maze.'

Febbs pressed the red button.

In the maze a tiny creature gave a yelp of horror.

Febbs jumped, startled. The tiny creature was roly-poly and adorable-looking. Somehow it was appealing even to him – and he normally detested animals, not to mention people. It began to hurry frantically through the maze, seeking the way out.

The placid telepathic voice continued. 'You will notice that this product, made for the domestic market and soon to be run off in quantity if it successfully passes such initial tests as you are providing it, bears a striking resemblance to the famous Empathic-Telepath Pseudononhomo Ludens Maze developed by Klug Enterprises and utilized recently as a weapon of war. Right?'

'Y-yes.' But his attention was still fixed on the travails of the tiny roly-poly creature. It was having a terrible time, becoming more confounded and more embroiled in the tortured ways and byways of the maze each second.

The harder it tried the deeper it became enmeshed. And

186

that's not right, Febbs thought – or rather felt. He *experienced* its torment, and that torment was appalling. Something had to be done about it, and now.

'Hey,' he said feebly. 'How do I get this animal, whatever it is, out?'

The telepathic voice informed him, 'On the left-hand side of the maze you will find a gaily-colored blue stud. Depress that stud, Mr. Febbs.'

Eagerly he pressed it.

He felt at once, or imagined he felt (which was it? The distinction seemed to have evaporated) a diminution of the terror surging within the trapped animal.

But almost at once that terror returned – and this time with renewed, even increased, severity.

'You would like,' the telepathic voice said, 'to get the man in the maze out. Would you not, Mr. Febbs? Be honest. Let's not kid ourselves. Is this not right?'

'Right,' Febbs whispered, nodding. 'But it's not a man, is it? I mean, it's just a bug or an animal or something. What *is* it?'

He needed to know. The answer was urgent to him. Maybe I can lift it out, he thought. Or yell to it. Somehow communicate with it so it sees how to get away and that I'm up here, trying for its sake.

'Hey!' he said to the scampering creature as it rebounded from one barrier to the next as the structure, the pattern, of the maze altered and realtered, always outwitting it. 'Who are you? What are you? Do you have a name?'

'I have a name,' the trapped creature thought back frantically to him, linking itself, its travails, with him. Sharing its plight with Surley G. Febbs desperately and gladly.

He felt himself emeshed now, not looking *down* at the maze from above but – seeing the barriers ahead of him, looming. He was —

He was the creature in the maze.

'My name,' he squealed, appealing to the enormous, not fully-understood entity above him whose countenance, whose presence, he had sensed for a moment ... but now who seemed

187

to be gone. He could no longer locate it. He was alone again as he faced the shifting walls on every side.

'My name,' he squealed, 'is Surley G. Febbs and I want to get out! Can you hear me, whoever you are up there? Can you *do* something for me?'

There was no answer. There was nothing, no one, above.

He scampered on alone.

THIRTY-THREE

At five-thirty that morning, still at his work-desk within his own conapt, Don Packard, the chief KACH-man from Division Seventeen of New York City, dictated with microphone in hand the memoranda which would comprise the documents served during the now beginning day of ordinary, normal men and women.

'With regard to the conspiracy composed of the six recently-added concomodies to the UN-W Natsec Board,' he declared into the mike, and paused briefly for a sip of coffee. 'That conspiratorial organization no longer exists. Its five members have been barbarously exterminated by the leader, S. G. Febbs. Febbs himself is now in a state of permanently induced psychotic withdrawal.'

Although this was the information which the client, General George Nitz wanted, it did not seem sufficient. So Don Packard amplified.

'At eleven o'clock a.m. yesterday, May 12, 2004, as revealed by KACH's several monitoring devices, the conspirators met in subsurface conapt 2A of Festung, Washington, D.C. building 507969584. This was their fourth meeting but the first and only time each of the concomodies brought with him/her the component from weapon item 401.

'I will not list the names of the six conspirators inasmuch as their names are already known to the Board.

'Reassembly of weapon item 401, which is the first non-*b* weapon of the new variant line, was begun by S. G. Febbs utilizing essential precision tools purchased at enormous cost.

'While reassembling the weapon item 401 S. G. Febbs outlined to his fellow conspirators the political and economic basis of the radical new system which he proposed to erect in place of the old, including the assassinations of well-known public figures.'

Pausing once more, Don Packard sipped more coffee. Then resumed his dictation, which, as he spoke it, was being autonomically transcribed into written document form by the apparatus before him.

'At four p.m. an ordinary 'stant mail robot delivered a plain-wrapped registered parcel to apartment 28 of conapt building 507969584. S. G. Febbs accepted the parcel and without opening it resumed his reassembling of the weapon.

'When the reassembly was completed, S. G. Febbs, as I have already stated (supra), exterminated these five co-conspirators, leaving only himself in possession of a now-proven, working model of weapon 401, the sole working model known to exist.'

Again Don Packard paused for more coffee. He was tired, but his job was almost over. Then he would carry a copy of the document now being dictated to General Nitz. It was all routine.

Packard wound up: 'S. G. Febbs fell victim to the Empathic-Telepathic whatever-it's-called Maze and shortly succumbed – in fact in record time, beating the smallest period established by voluntary prisoners from the Wes-bloc federal pen on Callisto.

'S. G. Febbs,' he declared into the mike in conclusion, 'is now at Wallingford Clinic, where he will remain indefinitely. However —'

At this point he broke off dictation and stared thoughtfully at his coffee cup. Since General Nitz was his client in this matter, Don Packard concluded his report with a footnote of his observations.

'It would seem,' he began thoughtfully, 'that since, due to the recent Emergency, Vincent Klug now has continual, legal access to the uniquely enormous autofac network of Lanferman Associates of California, and can run off in any quantity he wishes these damn mazes altered from the original weapon which was so effective against the aliens from Sirius, it might well be expedient to serve on Vincent Klug the instrument which has aided the Board so greatly in the past: an honorary but absolutely legally-binding commission in the Wes-bloc armed forces. Thus, should the need ever arrive —'

He paused once more, but this time not voluntarily.

The doorbell of his high-rent, high-rise, unlisted conapt had incredibly rung, and at not quite six a.m. Weird hour.

Well, it undoubtedly was a messenger from the Board, anxious to receive his report on the conspiracy of the six concomodies.

It was not, however, a military aide who faced him. In the hall stood a spic-and-span-new shiny 'stant mail delivery robot, with an ordinary-wrapped brown-paper parcel under its arm.

'Mr. Don Packard? I have a registered parcel for you.'

What the hell is it now? Packard asked himself irritably. Just when at last, he was about to knock off for the night and get some rest.

'Sign here,' the 'stant mail robot said, 'if you are Mr. Packard or if not Mr. Packard then on line two instead.' It presented a form, pen and flat surface of itself on which to jot.

Bleary-eyed, witless from a long night of ceaseless heavy work-load in which a good deal had happened, Don Packard of the private police agency KACH signed for and accepted the parcel. More monitoring or recording equipment, I suppose, he said to himself. They're always 'improving' these irritating technological contraptions which we have to lug around.

He carried the parcel grumpily back to his desk.

And opened it.

The world's greatest science fiction authors now available in Panther Books

Ray Bradbury

Fahrenheit 451	£1.95	☐
The Small Assassin	£1.50	☐
The October Country	£1.50	☐
The Illustrated Man	£1.95	☐
The Martian Chronicles	£1.95	☐
Dandelion Wine	£1.50	☐
The Golden Apples of the Sun	£1.95	☐
Something Wicked This Way Comes	£1.50	☐
The Machineries of Joy	£1.50	☐
Long After Midnight	£1.95	☐
The Stories of Ray Bradbury (Volume 1)	£2.95	☐
The Stories of Ray Bradbury (Volume 2)	£2.95	☐

Philip K Dick

Flow My Tears, The Policeman Said	£1.95	☐
Blade Runner (Do Androids Dream of Electric Sheep?)	£1.75	☐
Now Wait for Last Year	£1.95	☐
The Zap Gun	£1.95	☐
A Handful of Darkness	£1.50	☐
A Maze of Death	£1.50	☐
Ubik	£1.95	☐
Our Friends from Frolix 8	£1.95	☐
Clans of the Alphane Moon	£1.95	☐
The Transmigration of Timothy Archer	£1.95	☐
A Scanner Darkly	£1.95	☐
The Three Stigmata of Palmer Eldritch	£1.95	☐
The Penultimate Truth	£1.95	☐

To order direct from the publisher just tick the titles you want
and fill in the order form.

All these books are available at your local bookshop or newsagent, or can be ordered direct from the publisher..

To order direct from the publisher just tick the titles you want and fill in the form below.

Name _____

Address _____

_____

Send to:
Panther Cash Sales
PO Box 11, Falmouth, Cornwall TR10 9EN.

Please enclose remittance to the value of the cover price plus:

UK 45p for the first book, 20p for the second book plus 14p per copy for each additional book ordered to a maximum charge of £1.63.

BFPO and Eire 45p for the first book, 20p for the second book plus 14p per copy for the next 7 books, thereafter 8p per book.

Overseas 75p for the first book and 21p for each additional book.

Panther Books reserve the right to show new retail prices on covers, which may differ from those previously advertised in the text or elsewhere.